IF ONLY A HEART

And Other Tales of Terror

CALEB STEPHENS

Published in the United States by Salt Heart Press.
www.saltheartpress.com

Front & back cover image by Luke Spooner, Carrion House Illustration.
Book design by Molly Halstead.
Formatting by Molly Halstead.
Interior illustrations by P.L. McMillan.

First printing edition 2022.

https://www.calebstephensauthor.com/

PRAISE FOR *IF ONLY A HEART AND OTHER TALES OF TERROR*

"A captivating collection of creepy tales, infused with loss and pathos, about the most terrifying organ in the body—the human heart."

—Brian Asman, author of *Man, Fuck This House*

A cinematic roller-coaster of frightening fun. With steep drops into gory terror that leave you breathless, sharp curves that whiplash between heart and horror, Caleb Stephens' debut collection is an absolute thrill."

—C.B. Jones, author of *The Rules of the Road*

"*If Only A Heart* is a series of rich and vivid nightmares. Caleb Stephens powerfully weaves inhuman terrors into all-too-human tales of fraught relationships and personal suffering. Gorgeous prose. A breathtaking collection."

—Christi Nogle, author of *Beulah*

"Stephens is an emotional torture artist: he's jabbed my heart full of hooks, secured them with string, then played upon my fears like some pernicious puppeteer."

—Solomon Forse, editor of HOWL Society

"Caleb Stephens is a hell of a writer, certainly. But he's also a diabolical magician. In *If Only a Heart*, he populates his tales with characters so familiar at first glance, so seemingly comforting, you'd swear they were your own family, friends, neighbors... even yourself. But while you're distracted, he lets dread and terror seep in until they've sawed your heart in half. 'How'd he do it?' you ask; but it's too late, the next trick's about to begin."

—Patrick Barb, author of *Helicopter Parenting in the Age of Drone Warfare* and *Gargantuana's Ghost*

"*If Only A Heart*, at its core, has many stories that focus on family—found families, chosen yet unwanted families, families that are not actually family—and drags us on journeys that are filled with tension and often also with betrayal. Stephens frightens us with the cruelty of family, brings forth shudders when familial love does more harm than good—when a loved one cares perhaps just a little too much. Each story treads a fine balance, presenting the familiar idea of family as something uncanny, fearful, and dangerous when we expect safety instead. A chilling, heart-wrenching collection perfect for reading under the covers—but don't forget to come up for air."

—Ai Jiang, author of *Linghun*

"Caleb's stories in *If Only A Heart* are all parasitic worms aching to burrow into your skull meat to make a space of their own. Some are still slithering behind my eyes too, and I'm okay with that."

—Shane Hawk, author of *Anoka* and co-editor of *Never Whistle at Night*

CONTENTS

For Jen, always…

FOREWORD

Hello, dear reader! It is I, your friendly, neighbourhood P.L. McMillan coming at you hot. I've written short fiction, novellas, and blog on the regular, but this is my first foreword. Be gentle with me.

Caleb Stephens and I are friends by fate (a ka-tet of sorts). First, he was an editor for Hinnom Magazine, a cosmic horror publication in which a couple of my stories found a home. Then, without our realizing it, we had a few short stories published in the same anthologies. Finally, we were reunited when a story he wrote was selected for an anthology I was editing, *Howls from the Dark Ages*. What a ride! Now here we are: fast friends, and I am writing his foreword!

Having worked with him in so many different ways, one thing I've always admired about Caleb is his passion for his writing and his absolute drive to perfect his art. And not only is he always seeking out ways to improve his own craft, but he strives to uplift other writers and artists as well, forever providing encouragement and critiques. His natural storytelling ability, paired with his polished writing skill, makes this collection a tour de force.

With thirteen tales of terror, *If Only a Heart* will drown you in horror most monstrous, but also bury you under the weight of grief, loss, and guilt. Among the demons, shapeshifters, and Backward Men, are people struggling to live, to grow, to love.

In the following pages, Caleb explores what it means to be human – from the loss of a child, to the guilt of killing a close friend, to the blinding loyalty of brothers – this fiction will haunt you. Simply put, these thirteen stories are not for the faint of heart (bahdumtsh).

So get comfortable, dear reader, and prepare yourself. *If Only a Heart* is waiting…

…and it's hungry.

x P.L. McMillan
Author of *Sisters of the Crimson Vine*
plmcmillan.com

Yet who complains? My heart and I?
In this abundant earth no doubt
Is little room for things worn out:
Disdain them, break them, throw them by
And if before the days grew rough
We once were loved, used, — well enough,
I think, we've fared, my heart and I.

— Elizabeth Barrett Browning. "My Heart and I."

THE WALLPAPER MAN

We moved in a year ago. A month after Mom died. Just me and Dad and Piper and an old, salt-encrusted Victorian with big dormer windows and a swooping front porch. It's not much to look at, really. A faded-blue clapboard construction fronted by a piss-yellow lawn and a view of the Safeway parking lot across the street. Not exactly what I expected when Dad told me we were moving to the coast. He said he had to get away from her—or from the memory of her, anyway. Some bullshit line about missing her too much.

Nick, she haunts me. Every night, I can feel her in the room haunting me. It's not good for me here no more. Or for you and your sister. We need a fresh start somewhere else.

But I knew it wasn't a fresh start he needed. No, he wanted to run. I could see it in his nervous, washed-out eyes darting this way and that every time we went to the store, looking for the *I know what you did* looks. The tight smiles and curt nods in between all the poisoned glances. And at home, the trash cans boiling over with empty vodka bottles and crumpled cartons of Camel Lights, the floors ashed in dust. No one to clean them up anymore.

So, one day in late October, he pulled up in front of my school with a U-Haul tacked to the back of our rusted-out '98 Chevy Silverado, and we left. No warning. No time for goodbyes. Just a quick, "Get in, kid. I found us a place up the coast. A place we can get right again."

Piper cried the entire way. And me, well, I just bit my tongue.

The fear always starts in my toes when he speaks. A sinister prickle that blooms through my feet and spreads up my legs like a swarm of hatchling spiders in search of a meal. Some writhing, webbed-over treat to devour.

"I can helps you. I can makes it all go away."

The Wallpaper Man's voice is brittle, fluttering through the air of my room like a wisp of acrid smoke.

"Will it gives it to me? Will it gives me the pain?"

I shudder in my bed and pull the sheets higher, close my eyes, and hope to snuff it out, to drown it in the black void of my dreams—anything to make it stop, to make it go away.

Sometimes, when I'm feeling brave, I try to tune him out. I think about things like Piper's smile when I tell her one of my stupid knock-knock jokes. I love her smile. It's crooked-perfect just like Mom's was. I think about her, too. About her lavender perfume and how soft she felt when she hugged me. I miss those hugs. A *lot.*

When those things don't work, when I'm too afraid to think about anything else, I focus on the fear.

The color of it...black. *Definitely* black.

Its consistency...thick, like tree sap.

The taste...a bitter copper like when I bite my lip—like how I imagine battery acid would taste.

But it doesn't work. Nothing does. The Wallpaper Man is used to kids who can get out of bed. Kids who can run. Me, I have no use for legs. The ALS took them six months ago.

Most people are nice enough when they see me. I mean, sure, they stare a little too long and nod a little too hard when they say hello. They're quick to flash me a plastic smile and talk to me like I'm dumb or something. Like I'm a two-year-old, which I'm not. I'm sixteen. I just look young.

Whatever. I can't say I blame them. Who wants to spend time talking to death warmed over in a wheelchair? I sure as hell wouldn't. I mean, I can't bear to look at myself in the mirror. And why should I? I know how I look. The right side of my face droops like a stroke victim's, muscles frozen in place and not quite working right, with the other half scrunching tight like I just swallowed a mouthful of sour candy. My eyes are buried in sharp sockets, and my mouse-brown hair sprouts from my head in weird directions that don't quite make sense no matter how hard I try to smooth it into place.

The worst part is the pain. It's my entire existence. Cramps that go on forever. Muscle spasms and skin sores on my legs. Knees and elbows that lock up like rusty old latches.

Despite this, like I said, most people are nice.

Everyone except Roger Ellis.

I'm in the boys' bathroom, changing my catheter before first period, when the door bangs open to a cloud of Polo Sport and a heavy set of footsteps. I know it's him before he even speaks.

"Hey! Look who we have here. It's Nicky Twitch!"

Twitch—because it's what my body does.

"Leave me alone, Roger," I mutter.

Before I have a chance to brace myself, he's behind me—whipping my wheelchair around in a circle, whooping and sending the contents of my catheter bag all over my lap. The sharp smell of ammonia stings my nostrils as I swipe at my jeans with a nearby paper towel, hoping to mop it up before it soaks in.

"Hey, don't freak out, Twitch," Roger says, rounding my wheelchair. "I'm just messing with you, man. Looks like someone needs to cheer…" The words trail off, the corners of his mouth tugging into an evil grin. "Oh, my God. Did you piss yourself? You *did*, *didn't* you?" He barks out a laugh. "That's *so* disgusting. Wait until everyone hears about this. Pissing your pants! What a baby." He spouts a few more jags of laughter and stomps out of the bathroom.

I watch him go, rage swamping my chest, my lungs.

Roger has everything.

Perfect bone structure. Broad shoulders. A strong jawline already sprouting stubble. Girls chasing him everywhere he goes. He even drives a red Dodge Charger, one his lawyer father bought him the day he turned sixteen.

It's not fair.

He's everything I want to be, and everything I hate.

A ray of moonlight cuts through the blinds and washes over the wallpaper of my room. It's awful stuff: toy bears marching with trumpets, leading a troupe of stuffed animals through a candy-cane forest. Rabbits and deer and bug-eyed badgers following behind in a drunken zig-zag line, each wielding an instrument of their own. Rippling beneath it like he's floating in a pool of oil is the Wallpaper Man.

He has ten-inch serrated fingers that fall past a set of disjointed knees. His angular shoulder blades slope up into a razor-blade neck. His skull is long and segmented, punctuated by a jaw that curls inward, bones crackling when he speaks. Ridged eye sockets bulge from either side of his head and shift when he moves.

Four eyes in all.

I wish I could see *all* of him. Somehow it's worse being forced to picture the true horror that lies beneath the wallpaper. The slick rows of teeth that sometimes flicker against it when he speaks. The skin I imagine to be thick and black and reptilian.

"Has it brought me a name? Has it brought me the first of three?" His putrid breath seeps through the wallpaper, foul exhalations awaiting my response. "Gives me three names, and I will takes the pain, yesh?"

Night after night, it's the same question: *Will I give him his gifts? Will I give him his three names?* And night after night, I croak out a wet-gurgled *no*, my voice nothing more than a splash of baby vomit. I don't know what will happen if I give him a name. I don't want him to hurt anyone. But tonight, something's different.

Tonight, something cold boils through my blood at the prospect of having to face another day with Roger Ellis in it. Without thinking, I whisper his name.

I expect to see Roger slouched low at his desk the next morning, but it sits wonderfully empty. The sight fills me with relief. For the first time in a very long time, I can breathe. No looking over my shoulder, at least for today.

And it only gets better. He doesn't come to school the next day. Or the next.

It isn't until Friday that I start to worry.

Is he *dead*? Surely not, right? I didn't want to kill him, only hurt him a little…make him pay for everything he's done to me. Make him feel, I don't know, as worthless as I feel sometimes.

He comes to school on Monday and sits with his head cupped in his hands. He doesn't bother to look up when I enter class, a thick swoop of sweat-drenched hair obscuring his eyes. His foot taps out an irregular beat on the floor—a frantic *tap! tap! tap!*—that sends me rolling to my desk a little faster. As I glide past him, a burst of air pushes through his lips. It's laced with a familiar odor that tickles my nose.

The sticky tack of glue fumes.

I watch him throughout the entire class. There's something off about the way he sits, hunched forward like an eighty-year-old suffering from a lifetime of poor posture. His skin has taken on a strange chalky texture; it looks like drywall, like it would crumble beneath my fingertips if touched.

Halfway through class, he turns, his gaze locking with mine until I look away. For some reason, I expected to see anger in his eyes, for him to know this was my fault, that I did this to him. But what I saw staring back at me just now wasn't anger.

It was fear.

A lake of it.

Cold. Clear. Fear.

After the last period bell rings, I roll outside to the curb and wait for Dad to pick me up. It's frigid out. I shiver in my windbreaker and wonder how late he'll be today. Yesterday, it was half an hour. The day before, forty-five minutes and he was reeking of booze. If he's that late today, I'm pretty sure I'll freeze.

A shrill whine snaps me out of the thought. An ambulance. Distant, but coming closer. Then, behind me, I hear the cry. *Roger's* cry. It's pain-drenched and terrified. He's screaming like he's burning alive. I turn and spot him stumbling across the cement with two of his jock friends, his hands flapping like a pair of panicked birds, spraying watery-pink fluid everywhere. He collapses in front of me, a few feet away, and—Oh, God—his skin…

It's *gone*.

All of it.

In its place are pale bands of fibrous red muscle entwined with tangled nerve endings. Strips of bone peek through the pink tissue. And there's something else. Sticky white clumps of what look to be paste are speckled all over his ruined palms, coating his naked digits, running up to his forearms where the skin is peeling back in tattered strips.

I choke back a slug of bile.

The gym teacher, Mr. Johnson, abandons his post directing traffic and sprints over. "Jesus! What the hell happened here?"

One of Roger's friends, I think his name is Ethan, looks up wild-eyed, panicked. "It-it just—" He glances away and shakes his head. His eyes are wet. "His skin just came off, Mr. Johnson. Like a pair of gloves! We were playing catch, and Roger started screaming when he caught the football. We don't know what happened."

But I do.

I did this to him. I made this happen.

Roger unleashes a painful howl that slices through my ribcage all the way to my heart.

A moment later, the ambulance tears up to the curb, and I watch EMTs load Roger onto a stretcher, his eyes wild with pain, rotating in their sockets like dirty brown marbles as they wheel him away.

That night, my eyelids scrape open to sheer darkness. A tomb. I can't see the streetlight through my blinds, can't locate the reassuring red glow of my alarm clock on the dresser. My torso is slicked with sweat. I can't stop thinking about Roger's skin, about the way it peeled off his arms like paint left too long in the sun. The way it…

A chill washes down my arms, my legs.

Someone's watching me.

No, not some*one*.

Him.

My gums turn to sandpaper, my tongue swelling in my mouth. I can't handle him tonight. I can't give him another name and do this to someone else. I won't. I'll—

There's a knock at the door. "N-Nick? Are you awake?"

Piper.

My heart thrashes as the door creaks open. She can't come in here, not *now*.

Not with *him* here.

But, in more than a year, he's only ever talked to me, never Piper, and she needs me right now. I can feel the panic radiating off of her. Can hear it trembling in her ten-year-old voice.

"Hey there. You okay?" I ask.

"Can I sleep with you tonight?"

"Of course. Get in here." I lift the sheets and pat the bed. She used to sleep with me all the time when she was little, slipping into my room clutching her teddy bear while complaining about nightmares. But I knew that was a lie. She came in when the fighting got too rough, back when Dad would lose his temper with Mom, and the snap of his voice would pour through the house like dull claps of thunder.

I drape an arm around her as she slides in next to me and realize she's shivering.

"What's the matter? You have a bad dream or something?"

She shakes her head, a length of her hair tickling my chin.

"What then?"

"It was—" She shudders, lets out a sob.

"Go on. You can tell me. You know that, right?"

She nods, going quiet for a long moment before she says, "It was Dad. He was in my room again."

I stiffen, every wasted muscle in my body snapping taut. My throat glues itself shut as I run a hand over her head and soothe her until her breathing evens out. Then, I lie there wide awake and think of Mom lying dead-eyed on the bathroom floor, a storm of pills scattered around her lifeless fingers like fallen snowflakes. I think of the hem of her sweater hiked up just enough for me to see the purple patch of stomach peeking through, and the fist-sized bruises near her hip.

Dad always liked to keep his handiwork hidden.

I lie cardboard-stiff for hours, waiting…

And waiting…

Staring at the wall. Unable to sleep, willing him to appear.

Near three a.m., I finally catch a flicker of movement above my headrest, that familiar serriform grin bubbling to the surface.

A wallpaper talon extends from the wall, dipping gently to twirl a lock of Piper's hair.

"I like this one. Is this to be my gift? Is this to be my next name?"

"No," I reply, trying to steady my voice. "No, not her." *Never her.* "Someone else. I have your name."

In the morning, I wake Piper and have her wheel me into the kitchen, which has been outfitted for me—the one thing Dad's done right since we moved in. I make us a breakfast of scrambled eggs with sausage and orange juice and strawberry jam toast just like Mom used to. I even draw a smiley-face sunshine on Piper's napkin as I set the table.

It doesn't help.

We eat in silence, Piper barely touching her food—just pushing it around her plate while glancing at Dad's bedroom door off the kitchen like she expects it to burst open at any moment.

She stands a few minutes before the bus arrives and dons her backpack. As she turns to leave, I take hold of her arm and say, "Piper, that stuff with Dad, it's never going to happen again. Ever. You don't have to worry about him anymore, okay?"

Her eyes wilt, her lips pressing together in a thin line. She suddenly looks so like Mom with her chocolate-brown hair and her soft bubble of a nose, it hurts.

"Piper, I promise."

She gives me a quick nod, her eyes flicking to her feet, and I can tell she doesn't believe me.

After she leaves, after I tell her how much I love her, I stare at Dad's door for the longest time, my fingers vice-gripping the armrests of my wheelchair until my forearms feel like blocks of cement. Finally, after an hour, I roll over to knock once, twice, three times.

"Hello?"

I expect to hear his graveled voice telling me to fuck off, for him to yell at me to go away like he does every morning when I wake him up for my ride to school.

But no response comes.

Hesitantly, I turn the knob and roll into his room. Dust motes clutter the air, the carpet scattered with piles of dirty laundry: grease-stained tee-shirts intermixed with a bunch of torn jeans and crumpled polos.

An empty bottle of Jack Daniels lies cockeyed on his dresser, the room reeking like he hasn't opened a window in weeks.

"Dad?" I say, wheeling toward the bed.

And even though I can make out his form beneath the blankets, there's no answer. He just lies there motionless.

I call out again. More silence.

The last time I woke him from a whiskey-soaked bender, I got a black eye for my trouble—which is why I brace myself as I reach out and give his comforter a tug. It rustles down over something thin and fibrous, the sound like that of a grocery sack tearing. Only, what I find beneath is no grocery sack.

It's wallpaper. Miles of it.

The ugly brown and yellow striped stuff like on the walls of his room, winding from beneath his bed and running up and around his arms, his torso and legs. It covers his skull and forms a cup over his mouth. A long black stain leaks down the wall above his headboard, and his head is angled back toward it in a sick fashion that makes me think he saw it coming…whatever it was.

I find a crease in the wallpaper near his chest and take hold of it. Sprinkles of sand shiver through as I pull, streams of grit spilling onto the bed and scattering to the floor. I know I should stop, that I should turn and wheel myself out of the room, but I can't, my fingers working away as beads of sweat erupt across my forehead, my back. And then I'm ripping the wallpaper off in chunks, tearing into it like a toddler on Christmas morning who's anxious for his shiny new toy. Except what I find beneath is anything but shiny. All that's left of him is a pile of bones half-buried in sand, no flesh, no organs.

Nausea churns through my intestines, and I nearly retch, but somehow I manage to keep ripping and tearing, uncovering the remains of a pitted femur and the small bones of his wrist.

His skull.

It's bleached white, the eye sockets two black pits of tar peeking through all the matted grit.

After a while, I don't know how long, I turn and roll out of the room. Drifts of sand crunch beneath my wheels, my stomach spasming with disgust mixed with a sick satisfaction that it's finally over. Piper never has to worry about him again.

Piper. It hits me like a brick to the face. The Wallpaper Man won't stop without a third name, and I know who he wants.

The thought sends waves of gooseflesh rippling down my arms. It can't happen, and I won't let it. I have his final name. I've had it all along.

But first I need to make a call.

I wait for hours, the house creaking around me as I sit in the silence of my room, staring at the wallpaper. Dad promised me he'd take it down when we moved in. He said to give him a couple of weeks to get settled first.

Yeah, right.

Decayed fragments of light spill past the curtains onto the carpet. It's getting late. Aunt Lauren will be here soon. I can't wait any longer. One look at her, at the face so like Mom's, and all the strength will run out of me.

From my lap, I take the steak knife and press it against the heel of my palm until I feel the cold metal bite into my skin. Moisture frames my vision. I don't *want* to do this. I don't want to *die*, even if I don't have that long left to live as it is. The thought of never seeing Piper smile again, of never hearing her laugh or watching her wave at me from her bike, never again telling her how much I love her, is almost more than I can bear.

It's okay, though. Aunt Lauren loves Piper almost as much as I do. She'll take good care of her. Better than I ever could. She'll protect her. She'll give her the childhood she deserves.

I steel myself and slide the blade the length of my lifeline. The pain is indescribable—I'm gritting my teeth so hard that it feels as if my molars will crack—but I manage to keep it together long enough to roll over to the wall and press my hand against the wallpaper.

Work. Please, work.

I say my name.

Nothing happens. I can feel the blood pulsing out of the wound in thick torrents, turning the wallpaper sticky and slick. I struggle to focus, whispering my name over and over again.

"Take me."

My hand slips an inch.

"Please…"

Two inches.

My vision is failing, everything turning black.

A sudden, piercing cold floods my arm, and I look down to see Wallpaper-coated fingers encircling my wrist.

"I takes the pain, yes?" the Wallpaper Man asks.

"Yes," I reply.

"Yessshhhh." The hiss is otherworldly as it reverberates through my chest and washes down my legs in aching, undulating bursts. The fingers release their grip, and I thump back into my chair—unable to move, unable to blink. I can only stare dumbly at the ring of crusted black skin flaking off beneath my palm where the Wallpaper Man held me. I've never known pain like this before; it feels like I'm holding my hand in a hot pan of bacon grease.

A sheering sound brings my attention back to the wall. There, a single talon cuts a clean, vertical line through the vinyl paper. From the rift, it emerges, followed by another, and another, so many talons spilling through that I lose count. At least a dozen in all, maybe more. Beneath them, are fingers with black, knotted knuckles, impossibly long as they unfurl like the legs of some enormous spider.

"I takes the pain. I takes it *alllll.*"

The words carry with them a noxious rot that coats my nostrils and sets my eyes to watering. I blink through the tears and stare dumbfounded at the hundreds of miniature patches of wallpaper tearing away from the wall and migrating toward the hand, crawling like maggots onto the beetle-black palm. Shining trails of mucous mark their paths. They writhe and contort and twist upon one another in sick, disjointed motions, combining to sprout wings and antennae and hungry, sucking mouths.

I watch in disgust, unable to avert my eyes from the seizing horde as it convulses into something I recognize.

Moths. Dozens and dozens of wallpaper moths.

Another burst of decay spills from the wall, and before I can make a sound, they take flight and hurtle toward me, their razor-sharp wings lashing against my skin and their stabbing legs piercing my flesh. They work their rotten bodies into my mouth and down my throat, burrowing into my stomach, into the soft gelatin of my eyeballs. Pure agony swims through every cell of my being, my life spilling out of me in a thousand cuts at once.

Gray. White.

Muted, colorless shades.

I am everything, everywhere, all at once.

Flicking into existence in a new body. One that feels strange and electric and without pain.

One that feels dangerous.

I'm in a girl's room. I can tell by the mountain of stuffed animals bulging from the corner hammock: dogs and cats and a red-lipped, smiling monkey. A jewelry case rests on a white dresser. Posters of boy bands and horses speckle the walls. A tangle of beaded necklaces is draped over a rocking chair, and in the corner, from beneath a plush bedspread, a lush spray of hair drifts over a pillow. It's hard to see the color clearly through the striped wallpaper—it's dark—maybe amber, maybe brown. I can't quite tell with my new eyes.

All four of them.

DON'T LET HER IN

I hate my name, especially when Mom says it. *Nat.* It makes me think of gnats. Like I'm this annoying insect she wants to swat away anytime I say something.

Not now, Nat. Go away, Nat. I'm busy, Nat.

That's what I am to her—an annoying buzz at best. The kids at school are worse. They call me Fatilie, which I guess sorta makes sense. I mean, I *am* on the chunky side and all, but you'd think they'd be a little more creative with it...Fatilie is just so on the nose. Or maybe you wouldn't. I don't know. Most high school kids are pretty dumb.

The only person who's ever said my name in a way I liked was Grans. *Natalie.* She made it sound so beautiful, so natural. Like, *Here you go, Natalie, let me show you why your mother gave you this name.* We'd be cuddled up on the couch, wrapped in a couple of blankets while watching some movie, and she'd squeeze my knee and say something like, *Oh, Natalie, don't you just love this?*

And that's the thing. I truly did. To her, I wasn't this awkward fat girl trying to fit in, or the irritating daughter who was always in the way. I was just me, Natalie, and that was good enough for her. Not that it matters anymore. My sweet Grans died of dementia a year ago. She forgot my name entirely. To her, I became another stranger, and just like that, I was alone again.

"Are we getting close?" I asked, rubbing my eyes and sitting up. The rain was really coming down now, obscuring the palm trees lining the road and turning them into thin black giants whipping sideways in the wind. It was only half-past-five, but it might as well have been dusk with how thick the clouds were. Summer in Florida—you never knew when a thunderstorm would blow in.

"Mm, maybe another half-hour or so if this keeps up." Mom snatched her pack of Newports from the dash and shook out a cigarette, then lit it with a quick flick of her Bic. "You know, I'm getting sick of carting you around everywhere, Nat. You're seventeen. You should have your driver's license by now, don't you think? All your friends do."

"I don't have any friends."

"That's not true. What about Ashley? Oh, and that girl, Gina? The cute one I saw you talking to the other day after school."

"Ashley and I haven't been friends since freshman year, Mom. And Gina is my lab partner. She hates me."

And she does. Most of the kids at school do. Well, maybe not hate so much as ignore. I'm mostly invisible. I like to make a game out of it and see how long it takes for someone to acknowledge me. My record is four days, but I'm pretty sure I can make it a week if I really try.

Mom cracked her window and blew a stream of smoke into the rain. "My mother never drove me anywhere. If I wanted to go somewhere, I had to walk."

I didn't say anything. Just hearing her mention Grans made me sad.

"Look, either you get your license or your dad can come get you on his weekends. I'm done driving you down here. It's too far, and, unlike him, I actually have to work in the morn—Shit!"

I didn't have time to see what she saw. All I knew was that my head was fine one moment and flying toward the dash the next. I don't remember what followed except for a bunch of stars exploding behind my eyelids. After a moment, Mom's voice leaked into my ears, sounding muffled and tinny.

"...*was* that?"

I groaned and sat up. "Huh?"

"I said, what was—Oh, Lord, baby, you're bleeding." Her fingers wound past my bangs and prodded my forehead.

"Ouch," I said, slapping her hand away.

"Goddamn thing is supposed to have airbags. That's what Lew told me when I bought it from him, anyway, that lying bastard. Here," Mom said, digging into the console. "Let me get you a bandage. I have one in here some...where..."

The word hung there, her gaze back on the windshield. I followed it and went stiff. We were stopped on the shoulder of the highway, nearly in the ditch, and there was something on the hood. A *big* something, lying on its side with shattered legs extending from its body in odd angles. It had dark globe eyes and a long, broad jaw split by a row of ivory teeth. A deer, but larger, and not really a deer at all. It looked like...

"An elk," Mom muttered. "I think we hit an elk."

"But...there aren't any elk in Florida, are there?"

"I don't think so. I've certainly never seen one."

I fingered my forehead and winced. Mom dug her phone from her purse and punched in a number. I didn't hear a word of what she said, not with her voice coming out in a dull *mwah, mwah, mwah.* I just stared at the elk. It was huge. I mean, absolutely massive with these broad, muscular shoulders and a head that took up half the hood. Larger than any animal I'd ever seen, that was for sure—even bigger than the gators with the fat bellies I sometimes spotted sunbathing down near Miller Pond. And it was beautiful, that was the sad thing. Its coat was a rich, smooth brown, and it had a pair of antlers that spread out like a crown, the tips piercing the windshield in spots. Now it was dead, and we'd been the ones to kill it.

Mom set her phone on the dash. "They're sending a tow truck. It should be here soon."

Except it wouldn't. Ask anyone who knows. Steinhatchee, Florida, is pretty much the definition of the Middle of Nowhere. And we weren't even there yet, so this was worse than the Middle of Nowhere. I was pretty sure we were still somewhere near the tide swamp based on all the sawgrass jutting up across the road and the thick wall of chokeberry beyond it. I hadn't seen a streetlight for miles. I was just about to tell Mom as much when a low grunt filtered through the rain.

"Did it just…?" Mom asked.

"Uh, I think so." I tilted my head to get a better look. I could make out the elk's eyes. Eyes that snapped open and shut.

A scream lodged in my throat. "Did you see that?"

"See what?"

"It blinked."

Mom leaned closer. "I don't know, Nat. We hit it so hard. I'd be surprised if it was still alive."

An antler twitched.

"Oh," Mom said.

A sudden vibration shook the car, and then the elk was moving, coming to life in a series of jerks and heaves, its antlers rising and its legs wobbling like a newborn calf's. It planted one hoof on the hood, and then another, its knees bulging, somehow clicking back into place along with its legs. Legs that had been broken a moment earlier...the bones torquing beneath the skin, fusing into two straight lines with a series of uneven pops that made my stomach twist.

The car groaned beneath the thing's weight as it stood, and, for a moment, I thought the elk was going to bound off into the swamp like nothing had happened. But then its hindquarters jittered, and it tumbled off the hood and onto the road, where we couldn't see it.

I looked at Mom.

Mom looked at me.

And we sat there, staring at each other framed in the light bleeding from the dashboard, wondering what the hell had just happened. Through the holes in the windshield, we could hear the rain hissing against the hood, whooshing off the leaves and into the deep pockets of mud tucked behind the trees. The sound reminded me of the ocean before a storm—a bunch of angry water churning against the rocks. And something else. A noise out of place. That same grinding pop of bone from seconds earlier, only coming louder now, sounding like a hailstorm on a tin roof. Sounding like gunshots.

And then, with a lurching heave, the elk stood.

Except it wasn't an elk.

It was Grans.

"Dear God," Mom whispered.

I'd only seen Grans naked once before. I'd been six, maybe seven, at her house for a sleepover, when I'd accidentally walked into her bathroom without knocking. There she'd been, humming and drying her hair with an interstate of blue lines snaking down her thighs. Her breasts sagging and worn, ending in a set of nipples that pointed toward her thighs. It was one of those images that had scorched itself into my brain and stayed there. *So, this is what it looks like to get old.* I'd stood frozen in the doorway, hypnotized by the sight, until she yelped and escorted me back into the hall. *Now, now, Natalie, we always knock.*

That was exactly how I felt now, frozen. Mom, too, with both of us gawking at Grans, who was staring right back, steaming naked in the headlights with patches of fur clinging to her chest and neck. Grans, who was a year dead now—no, more than a year, somewhere closer to eighteen months—outlined in the headlights in perfect detail, just like on the day I'd walked in on her in that bathroom. Except, unlike that day, she didn't bother to cover up. She just stood there with her head cocked to the side and her mop-water-colored hair clinging to her face in strips.

After a moment, her mouth moved. And even though I couldn't hear her, I knew exactly what she said.

Natalie.

Mom yipped and grabbed her phone, hit the flashlight, and shined it past me through the windshield at Grans...who was gone.

"Christ, what's happening?" she asked.

"I don't know."

Grans' hand smacked my window, and I nearly swallowed my tongue as Mom aimed the light at her face. She gave us a sad smile and said something, her voice muffled behind the glass. But it *was* Grans' voice. It had the same inflection. The same tone. She motioned for me to roll down the window with a little turn of her wrist, and I found my hand drifting for the switch automatically—*yes ma'am*—the glass descending an inch before Mom grabbed my arm.

"Nat, wait."

"There she is," Grans said. "There's my sweet girl."

"Grans?" I blubbered.

She gave a little nod, and her smile broadened. I didn't know if it was me or the light, but her teeth seemed a shade darker than I remembered, like they'd been soaked in butter. "Yes, sweetheart. It's me. I've missed you. I've missed you so much."

"B-but how?" I stuttered.

Her face dropped, her mouth twisting to the side for a moment before her eyes found mine again and wilted.

"It's not true what they say, Natalie. About what happens after you die. The place you go, it's...it's not a good place. It's not nice. The things they do to you there..." Her voice fell a register. "Well, they hurt."

Mom moaned, and Grans nodded as if in agreement, as if that sound about summed it up, whatever it was she'd endured for the last year and a half.

"I couldn't stay there any longer. Especially not with how much you needed me. What kind of grandma would I be if I abandoned you, Natalie?" Pebbles of gooseflesh rippled across her chest. She rubbed her arms. "Be a dear and let me in, will you?" She nodded at the door handle as if deciding for me. "It's so cold out here."

My hand moved.

"Nat, *don't*." Mom's words came out in a hiss. I paused and looked at her. She shook her head once. "It's not her."

"How do you know?" I whispered.

"It's just—" Her eyes flicked past my shoulder. "It's just not, okay? Grans is dead."

"Oh, Jolene," Grans said with a sigh. "Didn't I raise you better than to leave an old woman standing out in the rain? And naked, no less. Where are your manners?"

I turned back to Grans, but she wasn't looking at me anymore. She was focused on Mom, her eyes burning.

"Jolene, you will let me in this car this *instant*, do you understand? This instant. Lord knows I raised you better than this. You should be ashamed of yourself."

Mom winced. "No. No, it's not you. You're not... I mean, Christ, Mom, you're *dead*."

Grans growled then, a strange clicking sound rolling up her throat. She straightened and worked down the fender toward the hood, looking unsteady, like she might trip and fall at any minute. Something burrowed beneath the strawberry-jelly-colored birthmark on her hip. It took a moment to place what, exactly, it reminded me of. And then it hit me. Snakes. Whatever was wriggling under her skin looked like snakes—a nest of long thin bodies that swam through her flesh like it was made of water.

"Start the car," I pleaded. "Start the car!"

Mom's hand jetted for the ignition and cranked the keys. The engine groaned and spit off waves of steam as Grans moved past the hood in the same old-woman walk that had consumed her before she'd died—shoulders stooped, one foot dragging behind the other. It was painful to watch.

"Help me!" she cried as she neared Mom's window. "I-I don't know where I am. Can...can you help me? Please, help me."

"Don't let her in," I begged.

Mom went for the window and tried to roll it up. Grans drew closer, the window sticking as Grans bent lower and tipped her forehead against the glass.

"Oh, hello there, ma'am. I'm sorry to trouble you, but I'm afraid…I'm afraid I'm lost. My daughter lives around here somewhere. Her name is…her name is…"

"Jolene," Mom said. "Her name is Jolene."

"Jolene," she echoed as if thinking about it. "Yes, what a pretty name. I knew a Jolene once. She was—" She gave her head a hard shake and massaged her temples. Her eyes clouded over. She looked at Mom and smiled brightly. "Oh, hello there, young woman. I'm afraid I'm lost."

"Mom," I said, grabbing her wrist. "Mom, look at me."

She turned, breathing hard through her nose, her lips clamped together in a thin line. Behind her, Grans gripped the window and wheezed. Mom grimaced, and I took her hand.

"It's not her. It's not. You said so yourself."

She nodded, but I could tell she was coming apart. Grans coughed again, and this time it left her in a long, wet hack with a rattle so deep that I felt it in my lungs. She wiped her mouth with the back of her hand, and it came away spotted in blood. Her brow furrowed as she looked at it, a string of spit leaking from her lip.

"I'm…not well. Where's my oxygen? I can't—I can't breathe. Please give me my oxygen, will you?"

Mom turned back to her. "I don't have your oxygen."

Grans slapped the window. "You have it in there, don't you, you little bitch? I know you do! You were always hiding things from me, Jolene. Always stealing my money and spending it on yourself. Buying all those fancy clothes, acting like you didn't take it, like it just grew legs and walked off on its own." Her eyes hardened. "You came out wrong, you know that? Even as a baby, you were hateful. Oh, the tantrums you threw, no matter how I tried to soothe you. You were always screaming, screaming, no matter what I did. I was never good enough for you."

"No, I-I..." Mom stuttered. "I never meant to—"

A sudden wash of light filled the car, dim at first and then growing brighter. I turned around, and my heart leaped. "Mom. Mom, look! Someone's coming." An SUV—or was it a truck? I couldn't tell—was easing to a stop ten yards back. The rain misted through the vehicle's headlights like twin swarms of mosquitos.

"Help us!" I shrieked. "Please, you have to help us!"

Mom was screaming, too, twisting around in her seat as Grans straightened next to her. I could no longer see her face, only a snatch of her blue-veined, mole-spotted torso. The snakes wriggled again, and the SUV blew past us in a great wheel of water. I watched the taillights disappear with a whimper.

Grans let loose another hack and lowered her face back to the window.

"I can't...I can't see anything." Her wheezing grew louder. Her fingers curled over the glass. "Help me. Please help me."

"Oh, Mom," Mom said, brushing the backs of Grans' knuckles with her fingertips.

Grans blinked. "Jo," she mumbled. "Jo, is that you?"

"Yes, Mom. It's me."

"Oh, punkin, I've been looking everywhere for you. Where have you been? Why won't you let me in? I'm freezing."

"I want to, Mom. I do, it's just—"

It was then I spotted Mom's hand near the door handle, one finger wrapped loosely around the silver latch, the latch that was tilting back, the lock popping...

"Mom!" I shouted, lurching for her too late. The door scissored open a crack, and Grans moved like a snake, darting and quick. She yanked the door open with one hand and grabbed Mom with the other. Mom snapped around to look at me with eyes that were wide and white.

"Nat—"

It was all she said before Grans wrenched her from the seat and into the storm.

I sat there for an awful moment. Stunned, unable to move, unable to think. I stared through the now wide-open door and was able to make out a rustle in the bushes across the road. A back-and-forth swish of palm fronds that didn't quite match the rhythm of the rain. A shriek rang out. Mom's shriek, followed by another. One that didn't sound human.

My heart fluttered in my chest. I scrambled for the door and yanked it shut, locked it, and fell back into my seat breathing hard. Hyperventilating. Spots swam through my vision. For a moment, I thought about running. For a big girl, I was pretty fast. But there was no way I'd be able to outrun whatever this thing was. Not when it had snatched Mom so quickly.

Grans' cry came again, and my bladder clenched in response. I didn't want to die. Suddenly, my life, shitty as it was, looked pretty good compared to the alternative. I wanted to be back home in my bed, buried beneath the covers. I wanted to shut my eyes and pretend this was all a bad dream.

But it wasn't.

And I was next.

It didn't take long for Grans to return, that clicking noise I'd heard earlier working its way toward me through the thrashing rain. It sounded like one of the velociraptors from *Jurassic Park*. Like death. When she landed on the hood in a crouch, I nearly peed myself. She swayed in front of the windshield with eyes that were no longer colored, but fully black. Inky webs of rainwater bled from the corners. Dark fluid stained the creases of her nose. Her jaw was a mess of blood, as was her chest. She made no motion to wipe it away. The rain did it for her. She just remained crouched there, looking at me like I was a lab rat. Like I was the one on display even though she was the naked one. Even though I could see raindrops leaking off the sparse triangle of pubic hair between her thighs.

She smiled and licked her teeth. "Be a good girl, Natalie. Come give your Grans some sugar."

My stomach churned. I didn't move an inch. It was a line from my childhood. Something she'd say after buying me an ice cream cone or a pack of Mike and Ike's for a Saturday matinee. I'd thank her, and she'd bring her cheek low and pat it once, twice. *Come give your Grans some sugar.*

"Now, now, Natalie," she said. "You can't stay in there forever. I'll get you out sooner or later. We can do it the easy way or—" Her smile widened. "Well, you know."

"Go away," I whispered. "Please, just go away."

She let out a long, slow sigh. "You always were a stubborn one, weren't you? You got that nasty little trait from your mother."

I didn't have time to respond before she slammed her head against the windshield. The glass splintered. She struck again, and again, the window spider-webbing wider with each *crunch! crunch! crunch!* Then, her hand was through and reaching for me. Blood wound down her arm as it stretched past the dash and over the seat, all the way to my neck. It paused and rose higher, the pads of her fingers brushing tenderly over my jaw, my ears.

"How I've missed you, Natalie."

I wanted it to be her. I'd never wanted something more. But it wasn't.

I squelched my eyes shut and shook my head. "You're not her. You're not my Grans."

"No, but I'm close enough."

Her fingers dug into my neck, then wound entirely around it. I heard her knuckles creak and groan. I gasped for air, fighting until my vision blurred and my pulse thumped in my ears. The last thing I'd remember was the roar of an engine coming from… somewhere. Of cold halogen filling the cabin along with the smell of exhaust. And then I was gone.

The deep chug of pistons and diesel woke me, followed by a light pressure on my shoulder, a weight that felt like a hand.

Deasy. Hay tay gud deasy.

Grans' hand.

I snapped upright and dug my nails into warm flesh.

"Where is she?" I asked. "The old lady. Tell me she's gone. Did you see her? Or my mom? Where's my mom?"

"Ouch, shit. Jesus," a deep voice said. "Take it easy. You're fine. Y'all called for a tow, right?"

I rubbed my eyes and tried to clear the haze. The man came into focus: a dim shadow sitting behind the wheel of a truck, a toothpick working out from beneath a thick mustache. In front of him, through a windshield streaked in dust and a field of dead insects, the night road washed away, devoured by a pair of headlights.

"Look, sweetheart," the man continued, "I don't know what sorta trouble y'all got into out here, but you were the only one in that car when I showed up. And you weren't looking so hot. I thought about calling for an ambulance, but you looked bad enough that I figured I'd better get you to the hospital myself."

I snatched his arm. "We have to go back. We were attacked. There was this *thing*. My mom, she, she—" My throat swelled. I buried my face in my hands. "Oh my God, she's dead."

"Whoa," the man said. "C'mon, now. Don't do that to yourself. I called the police the minute I showed up. They'll be there shortly. They'll find your mom. I'm sure she just wandered off somewhere. It happens sometimes with head injuries. You just rest up and—"

The sound of the tires slamming up against the wheel wells drowned him out, a sick thud followed by a dry crunch. The truck's air brakes popped with a steady *psss*.

"Holy hell, that deer came out of nowhere! I've never seen one move that fast bef…"

He trailed off, staring at something beyond the windshield. I followed his gaze and sucked in a breath. There was a girl standing in the middle of the road completely naked, maybe five if I were to guess, with flaxen hair and soft white skin. She had her hands clasped neatly at the waist.

"It can't be," he said.

"Who is that?" I asked.

The girl smiled, and he ran the back of his hand across his face and sniffed. "It's my daughter, but...she's dead."

A woozy wave of adrenaline flooded my veins. I leaned across the seat and yanked the man toward me by the collar of his shirt.

"Listen to me. That girl, that *thing* out there, isn't your daughter. Okay?"

His eyes brimmed with tears. His mouth hung slack.

"Please," I said, tightening my grip. "Don't look at her. Don't stop driving." I took a quick, shivery breath. "And whatever you do. Don't. Let. Her. In."

I WILL WAIT FOR YOU

You dig your fingernails into your wrist as you stare out the window and wait. A gust of wind whips bits of sand against the glass, scattering tracks of it over the pane, tracks like the red ones welling up beneath your fingertips. Outside, bright peals of laughter ring out. Costumes flash beneath a scatter of half-dead trees, orange pumpkin candy baskets bobbing like neon, spectral orbs. You *see* none of it, *hear* none of it—not the chimes of doorbells or the muffled "trick-or-treats." No, your grief holds you captive, here, at the window, like it does every year on this night. Waiting...

Waiting for her.

You glance again at the photograph clutched in your hand. Your daughter smiles back at you with those warm almond eyes so like yours, her freckles peppered in soft brown constellations over a pair of apple-slice cheeks. You trace your thumb across them and remember the feel of her skin on yours, her little body so vibrant, so bursting with life, you would have thought she'd live forever. She was your world, this girl, the very heart beating in your chest.

You tilt your gaze up and wait for the drifts of fog to creep in as they always do, those first few lonesome curls that set your pulse to crashing like the waves of some great storm against a rock-strewn coast. A woman bundled in a thick wool sweater strolls by with a wobbly bumblebee in tow, a girl of maybe four, both of them practically glowing, and you think, *I used to have that once...that other life.*

Then, you see it, a pale wisp of mist coiling around the branches of the laurel oak where you pushed your daughter on her rope swing—*Higher, Mommy! Higher!*—and you nearly forget to breathe. The fog thickens, settling over the lawn in blankets, great drifts of it rising until all that's left of the outside world is a faded charcoal imprint.

She appears in flashes, like something seen through a storm: a swell of chestnut hair, skin bleached the color of marble with eyes that are deep and black, the whites long since drowned. She carries the stuffed bear you won for her at the spring carnival, love-worn with one eye missing and the fur patched over in spots.

Your daughter nears the window and sets her hand upon it, and you reach out with yours, the pads of your fingertips trembling as you press them over hers. She's beautiful, a vision in the lace dress you buried her in—cream-colored and embroidered with lilacs, her favorite flower. Your eyes burn over every feature—her slender nose and the perfectly curved eyebrows. Her delicate cheekbones. Below, nestled in the cup of her collarbone, you glimpse the moon-shaped scar from the playground accident that sent her wailing into your arms when she was five, her breath brushing warm against your chest as you stroked her hair.

She mouths something through the glass, her lips forming a perfect blue circle. It's a word you know by heart.

"Mommy."

You nearly cry out because you want this moment to last forever, a lifetime, but you know it can't. You know what comes next.

"Mommy...where are you?" she asks, pressing her other hand to the glass. Her mirror-black eyes beg you to respond, to rush outside and fold her into your arms and tell her that you're here, that you're always *right* here.

And you've tried.

Thrashing against doorknobs that won't turn, screaming her name as you scratch the wood bloody. And the windows like concrete, your knuckles raw and bleeding as you hammer your fists into them over and over and over again. It doesn't matter. Nothing works. Nothing ever does. All you have is this moment, this brief, precious moment—here, now, once a year, looking through the glass.

Your daughter's face splinters into a mask of pain, and a sob you didn't know was building climbs your throat. Hot tears bleed down your cheeks as the first few threads of her hair unwind and float into the mist like fragile strands of spider silk. Then, more of it comes loose, dark chunks raining down just as they did with the chemo. Her skin pales and tightens around her skull like a sheet of cellophane, and you want to look away, *need* to look away, but you can't. You never do. She's your soul, and you live and die for this night.

Every single moment.

"Mommy...please. Where are you? Why is everything so dark..."

A rash breaks over her cheeks, veins spilling down her arms in little blue rivers, and the dam behind your eyes bursts. You rest your forehead against the windowpane with great heaving sobs, your heart scraping your chest as your daughter dissolves bit by awful bit. First her skin as it flakes to ash. Then her muscles, her bones, everything rising into the haze until all that's left of her is the delicate set of fingerprints she's left on the glass.

Tears patter off the windowsill, everything coming back into focus now as the fog recedes, pulling back as if sucked into the lungs of some giant creature hidden in the ether. The memory of her slides through your brain like a ribbon of smoke.

Your little girl. Your *life*.

Your hand is still on the window, still shaking, and you pull it back and stare once more into the gathering darkness. Jack-o'-lanterns line the street in warm gold flickers, the trees hanging above them like silent ghosts. You wipe your eyes, and, after a moment, whisper what you whisper every Halloween, the anniversary of the night you lost your daughter forever ten years earlier.

"I will wait for you. I will *always* wait for you."

IF ONLY A HEART

Paul cracked his eyes open to the weak, pre-dawn light of the tent and rolled toward his daughter, toward the bloom of cinnamon-colored hair that was so like Catherine's, it sometimes stopped his heart.

His hand drifted for her shoulder. "Morning. How'd you..."

The words dribbled off his tongue and died. Her sleeping bag was empty, the red nylon fabric wrinkled and overturned. He sat up, and his gaze fell upon the open tent flap and the gray wash of early morning sky beyond it.

She must be up already. He unzipped himself and stood to stretch. *She must have gone to pee.*

He fumbled a hoodie from his pack and pulled it on, this followed by his sweatpants and shoes, then pushed outside to a mix of wet earth and fog. In the distance, rising like a purple bruise from the lush green earth, was the spine of the Appalachians, and closer yet stood Mount Sequoyah, cloaked in a magnificent robe of red oak and pignut hickory. Today, finally, after a week on the trail, they'd spread Catherine's ashes on the summit and begin to heal.

He searched the campsite for Olivia and saw only the pair of logs they'd dragged next to their fire last night, surrounded by miles of dense thicket and brush, into which she must have slipped off to pee.

Off the beaten path. That's where Olivia had wanted to go. Somewhere she could escape the pain of losing her mother. It still hung on her a year later with the weight of a thousand-pound anchor. He saw it in the way her shoulders curled as she walked, and the way she never seemed to smile anymore; his daughter navigated life like a ship floating on a stretch of dead water, her despair threatening to pull her down, down, down…

Paul cupped his hands to his mouth and blew. *Off the beaten path.* And they were, sidetracked by at least a quarter-mile if he were to guess. Maybe more. They'd been diverted last night by a stray deer trail and the fading light. By the time he'd realized his error and brought them to a halt, it had been too late to turn around. Best to break for camp and wait for morning. He'd read too many stories of panicked hikers snapping bones at night, trying to find their way back to a trailhead or a parked car.

Stretching again, he listened for the sound of his daughter's twelve-year-old feet working over the wet leaves, heading back to camp. He should have heard something of her by now, a rustling in the brush or her giggle as she jumped out from behind a tree to scare him.

But there was nothing—no breeze, no birds—with everything as quiet as if it had been smothered in an inch of cotton.

He walked to the edge of the camp and called for her, bringing his hands up to yell, "Livvie, it's time for breakfast!"

There was no answer.

He called for her again, "Livvie! This isn't funny! Where are you?" A familiar knife of dread sliced down his spine, the same one that had impaled him every day since he'd lost Catherine—this vague feeling that the worst was still to come.

"LIVVIE!"

His voice echoed back faintly, swallowed by all the brush as he circled the camp, shouting out for her. He scanned the ground for her footprints, for any sign of her. There were none, just the forest floor covered in a blanket of pine needles interspersed with thick tangles of witch hazel. Then, he saw it—a fresh carving cut into the trunk of a sapling maple at the edge of camp.

It was a heart.

But not the ubiquitous curve of love he'd seen etched into the bark of so many neighborhood park trees. This heart was an actual...*heart*. Two atria. Two ventricles. Veins cutting exquisitely through cords of muscle that looked so lifelike he practically expected it to start beating.

How was it so detailed? He knew no blade could have carved this, or at least none wielded by a stray camper or two. It was far too intricate for that. And besides, who would spend the required amount of time to do such a thing, especially up here where nobody would see it?

He blinked and glanced lower, the air rushing out of him when he spotted a print stamped deep in the mud, with five...no, *six* toes tipped in claw marks. It was thin and bone-like—longer than any animal track he'd ever seen by at least half a foot. Another one angled deeper into the woods a few feet away. And another yet.

Paul burst into the thicket and ran.

"Don't you dare," Catherine said, slapping his hand away from the radio.

Paul laughed and withdrew it, consigning himself to another two hundred miles of listening to *Country Top 40*—which actually meant some annoying DJ playing the same five twangy songs on repeat.

Catherine rolled her eyes and looked back through the rain-spattered windshield toward the canyon of trees beyond, frosted by a gunmetal sky. "You really think she'll have fun?"

"I know she will."

"It's just...she's never been away from us this long before."

"I think it'll be harder on you."

"Probably."

He reached over and took her hand to give it a squeeze. "Livvie's a tough one. Like her mom. She'll be fine."

One look at Camp Klehani, and Paul had known Olivia would forget about them the second they left. The cabins were planted around a pristine lake and replete with all things summer camp: horseback riding, archery, soccer, rock climbing, and arts and crafts. The place was basically kid heaven.

"I hope so. She's growing up so fast." Her voice cracked on the last word. "I'm not ready for it."

Paul glanced her way. "Me neither." And he wasn't. Olivia *was* growing up too fast. It seemed like just yesterday that he'd bounced her on his knee as a toddler, those huge brown eyes of hers begging him for another bedtime story or a quick tickle. And now she was eleven? How had that happened?

"She'll be in middle school next year. *Middle school*. I just feel like...Paul, watch out!"

He brought his attention back to the road, too late, and jerked the wheel right to avoid the oncoming truck as it careened over the yellow line straight toward them. Then they were slamming down the hill, rocks and dirt and branches slapping at the glass before the car hit an expanse of cold, dead air.

He barreled downslope.

The bracken quickly thickened around him, tearing at his throat and arms, etching a highway of red tracks across his skin. He ignored the pain; it didn't matter.

His heart thundered with every step.

Livvie.

He couldn't lose her. Not after Catherine. Livvie was all that remained of her; the only thing that kept his ruined heart beating, and even then, just so.

Deadfall littered the path. There were piles of dead or decaying wood to navigate, walls of brush that were stitched together in thick knots with roots that devoured the soil and snagged his ankles at every turn. The forest seemed to grow around him, the trees towering twenty, thirty, a hundred feet overhead. Black-barked giants stretched for the sky everywhere he looked, trailing long strips of moss from their branches to the forest floor.

"LIVVIE!"

The world around him was one that shouldn't exist in Appalachia. He'd been on plenty of backpacking trips with Catherine before they'd married, the two of them sipping wine from red Solo cups with the stars sprinkled above them like diamonds cast from the hand of God.

They'd spent days out here, sometimes weeks, hiking through vast forests of spruce, sugar maple, birch, and white oak. They'd summited fog-shrouded peaks that gave view to miles of rolling green woodland carpet. And in all that time, he'd seen nothing remotely like this.

The light faded above him as the trees grew thick with a canopy of rot, the desiccated leaves curling in on themselves, falling around him so he could barely see the forest floor. The memory of Catherine's voice hissed in his ear. Her final request: *Protect her, Paul.*

"LIVVIE!"

He broke into a wide clearing spotted with waist-high clumps of grass and thick clusters of rhododendrons. At its center stood a structure that didn't make sense. A cabin, but not a cabin. Log beams erupted from the earth at impossible angles and curved into the frame in ways timber shouldn't move, in smooth bends and vicious, ninety-degree twists. Thin slat planks were pasted together in intersecting angles, climbing toward a patchwork roof. Windows pocked the exterior like they'd been placed there with all the care of a shotgun blast—some sitting sideways, some with frames that hung completely upside-down.

Acid splashed up his throat, and panic blurred his vision. He imagined Livvie chained somewhere inside, calling for him, screaming his name over and over without a response.

Stop it. Find the tracks.

He rubbed the moisture from his eyes and focused. It took him a moment, but he spotted them running ahead, cutting a subtle valley through the field of dense green blades surrounding the structure. He followed the path around the house, to the rear, where a broad set of flagstone steps ran lower toward a smooth steel door.

A deep vibration filled the earth as he descended, clouds of dust choking the air and obscuring the early morning light. He spun around and froze. The staircase now stretched impossibly high above him, at least a hundred steps or more, the sun slanting down through a swirling cloud of dust motes.

It wasn't possible.

With a hard swallow, he turned back to the door and examined it. There was no doorknob or knocker, nothing with which to open the dark iron slab. But there was a heart. The *same* heart that was carved into the tree near their tent stamped directly in its center. Something about the sight of it filled Paul with a terror so palpable, so *thick*, it tore the air from his lungs.

He raised a hand to knock and hesitated for a moment, then unwound his fist and pressed a single finger to the door. The others followed, his fingernails *click, click, clicking* down over the cool metal until his entire palm rested on the iron. Without warning, a wave of liquid fire tore up his arm like he'd cranked an oven burner to ten and set his palm upon the coils. Frantic, he jerked his hand back but it...

Wouldn't.

Fucking.

Move.

Paul stared as flares of acrid smoke curled from his fingertips, the meat of his palm crackling in front of his eyes like a greased strip of bacon. He could smell his flesh burning, could *taste* its sweet heat climbing into his nostrils. A scream he didn't recognize as his own ripped up his throat a second before he blacked out.

When he woke, he was sitting in some sort of...chamber, one draped in mirrors whose frames were encrusted with glittering, nameless jewels so bright, so retina-searing, that he could barely stand to look at them.

A tingling sensation filled his forearm, and he whipped his gaze down, expecting to see a pile of blackened skin. Instead, he saw a palm that was smooth and pink, secured by a pale, flesh-like restraint. His other hand was bound in a similar fashion, tied to a chair that wasn't just a chair, but something more. It stirred beneath him, radiating warmth, pulsing with a familiar rhythm…

A heartbeat.

Paul thrashed and tore at the restraints, the bands of flesh tightening with each movement, each terrified pull, the tension growing so great, it felt like his wrists would snap.

A cold paralysis filled him, followed by the feeling of being watched.

He searched for its source, his eyes wild, until he spotted a distortion in the center of the chamber, a black void where something stood with the air whirling around it like coils of smoke.

Movement bled from within, and there came the sound of joints snapping, of a spine straightening. The creature, whatever it was, rose and lumbered toward him in a swirl of murky light. Through it, Paul caught snatches of impossibly purple irises, and an elongated, mouthless jaw. Its limbs were draped in translucent flesh, its organs packed deep in its abdomen like fresh cuts of meat.

Cold sweat spackled the back of his neck.

"DADDY!"

Livvie's voice assaulted him from every direction, all at once. She stared back at him from every mirror—his little girl, her lips curved wide in fear.

Paul returned his attention to the thing with a growl.

"What do you want from me?"

In response, the creature raised its hand and traced a finger across Paul's forehead, and he slumped forward.

Water rushing.

Stones heaving.

And grinding.

The sensation of floating, followed by one of sinking.

A heavy, wet weight on his chest, encompassing his arms and pressing down.

"Paul. I-I can't...move."

Catherine's cough rose wretched and wet next to him, and he shot awake to a freezing pool of green water swirling around him, flecked with pockets of foam. He shook his head and tried to clear the cobwebs obscuring his vision. A warm red drizzle crept over his forehead and seeped into his eyes.

"Paul!"

Catherine. He pawed the blood from his vision and searched for her. There she sat with her head lying at an unnatural angle upon the dash. Her eyes were wide and panicked, and her nostrils flared with each labored breath. "H-help...me."

He came alive and tore off his seatbelt, then climbed clumsily over the center console toward her. His hands dove into the pool of freezing water at her waist, his fingers already so numb with cold, he couldn't feel the straps of her seatbelt threading toward the buckle.

"W-what happened?" she asked.

He ignored the question and pulled her buckle from the latch. She came loose in his arms, nothing but dead weight as he heaved her toward his door, stopping only when she cried out.

"My foot's caught. I can't... I—" she coughed, and a dark button of blood stained her lips. "I can't feel anything." Her eyes fluttered then, and he knew he was losing her.

He set his hand on her cheek. "Hey, I'm right here. Take a breath and tell me what hurts." *Jesus. Stay with me, Cat.*

She blinked again and gave him a slight nod, the river nearly to her chest now. Frantic, he sucked in a lungful of air and plunged beneath the icy water, felt down her leg to an angry snarl of metal and rubber. He pried at it, pulling on her leg until his lungs nearly burst and veins of white light bisected his vision. When he surfaced for a gulp of air, the water was at Catherine's chin, and her eyes were muddy and unfocused.

"Go," she said, her voice barely a whisper above the water's roar.

"No," Paul said, "I'm not leaving you!"

"You...h-have to. F-for Livvie."

Water bubbled past the windows and waterfalled down the doors. They were spinning now, sinking deeper.

His heart caught in his throat.

"Cat..."

Her eyes flared to life with a sudden, blinding intensity. "Protect her, Paul. Promise me you'll protect her. No matter what. Promise you'll protect Livvie."

"No, I told you, I'm not leav—"

"*Promise me!*"

And with his voice crumbling, he did.

"I can protect her. I can keep your promise."

The creature's inhuman voice tore into Paul like a shower of glass, sharp and piercingly bright, the tone slicing through the synapses of his brain like a thousand hungry razors. He strained against the chair that wasn't a chair and took a quick, stabbing breath.

"Your life. For hers."

The thing was speaking to him, but not with its mouth, for it had no mouth. Instead, the words bloomed inside of his skull and filled his head with a terrible pressure.

"Daddy, help me!"

A blinding rage tore through him at the sound of Livvie's voice, and he ripped at the restraints binding his forearms once more, putting all his remaining strength into breaking free and—

The crack of his wrist was instant and sharp. He fought for breath beneath the anguish, his bones splintering like brittle kindling as the restraint coiled tighter. "Why…are you doing this to me?" he groaned. "What do you want?"

The abomination leaned toward him and ran a translucent finger from his cheek down to his neck, and then lower toward his heart. It came to rest there with a single tap.

"Choose."

"Where are you, Daddy? I can't see anything. It's dark in here. I'm scared. So scared. Why won't you help me?"

He broke at that, picturing her as a little girl fresh from a nightmare, her face still creased with sleep. *Daddy's here, baby. You're safe now. You're safe...*

"Chooooose."

Paul gasped. The creature's voice ran through his veins like acid. The words burst up his throat unchecked: "Me! Take me, god damn you!"

The thing shuddered, an endless ocean of relief flooding from the creature and into Paul as it tore his shirt and spread it wide. A talon flicked across his chest, sending a hot sheet of blood spilling down his ribcage and onto his lap. Then, the talons were sinking deeper…

Cutting, cutting. So sharp.

Through his ribs and past his lungs.

Pressing deeper into his chest.

There came a heavy weight followed by a fatal ripping sensation, vital things inside of him giving way as the creature withdrew its hand. And clutched there, still beating, was *Paul's* heart.

Thump.

His. Fucking. Heart. *Th-thump. Thump.*

He gasped as a shredding sound filled the air, something like stitches popping, and the thing's translucent skin tore open to reveal the beginnings of a...*mouth.* A horrible wet semi-circle of white flesh that gave way to a long dark maw. The creature's jaw unhinged further, that awful crystalline skin continuing to tear and part until, to Paul's horror, it lifted his heart and placed it inside.

Then, he saw nothing at all.

The woman came into existence one frame at a time. A splash of color standing in the middle of a mirrored chamber. A woman in a yellow summer dress, wearing a smile that ran through him like a cold drink of water. Catherine was her name, but it *couldn't* be her. He'd lost her to the river. They'd dredged for days. Still, it *was* her, perched just a few feet away with an arm wrapped around something, no, some*one*.

A girl who was somehow important to him. *The* most important thing of all.

The girl's shoulders heaved when she spotted him, and the woman—he couldn't remember her name now—pulled her closer and whispered something in her ear.

Watching them, he felt a vague sensation of sinking, of being pulled lower, down, down, down...

Why couldn't he remember the girl's name?

Why couldn't he remember his own?

And his body—it felt so different, so strange.

He glanced down at his arm and felt his eyes widen in shock. His skin was clear, giving view to a dark forest of veins. He flexed his hand and stiffened when a set of talons curled in response. Revulsion burned up his spine. He looked toward the woman and tried to say something, *anything*, but he couldn't.

He no longer had lips, or a tongue.

The woman stared at him for a long moment, something sad in her eyes, and then took the girl's hand and led her away from him toward the mouth of a dark passage. There, she hesitated and turned to face him once more. Her irises seemed to blaze purple for a brief moment before fading to a rich hazel brown. It was a color that had once meant something to him. As had the girl.

But no more.

Now, nothing mattered.

Nothing but finding a heart.

WELCOME TO CAMP KLEHANI!

1986

I stare at the cheerfully carved letters tacked over the door and groan: Welcome To Camp Klehani!

Fat camp. Jesus...

I'd fought hard not to come, but I knew it was over the moment Mom got her hands on that glossy flier with the kid smiling down from an exercise bike like it was a rollercoaster. She'd been having whispered conversations about my weight with Dad for over a year now. I'd moved well beyond "big-boned" territory. Still, I'd thought the cost alone might save me from going. I mean, a thousand bucks is no joke, especially for a cheapo like Dad, but he'd agreed immediately.

Yay.

I slap at a mosquito with a stinger the size of a coffee straw and stroll into the lodge. A mounted deer head takes stock of me from the far wall, its dull, glass-bead eyes oozing disapproval.

"Name?" mutters a girl from a rickety folding table. She glances up as I lug my suitcase over, and my voice clogs. I've never seen someone so beautiful. A fountain of frizzy blonde curls spills over a purple scrunchie, her eyes an electric, ocean green. She looks like Heather Locklear, only prettier, with lips that sparkle beneath a thin layer of bubblegum-pink lip gloss. "Name?" she repeats.

"Um…Bobby. Bobby Bacon."

I hate my name, by the way.

She arches an eyebrow. "Seriously?"

A snort rises behind me. "Pfft, Bacon? At fat camp? You can't make this shit up!"

I turn toward a kid stuffed into a black *Metallica: Ride the Lightning* tank top. Well, "kid" isn't exactly the right word for him. He looks more like a man-child with a pair of honey-baked hams for arms and a massive gut bulging out over a ripped pair of Jordache jeans. A river of acne pocks his face, and he has a weak chin that's hard to differentiate from his neck.

In other words, he doesn't have a lot of room to be busting my balls.

"I'm just joshing you, man," he says, slapping my shoulder. "The name's Cody."

The counselor rolls her eyes. "Can we get a move on, guys? You're holding up the line."

It's true. I didn't hear them come in, but kids are piling up behind us, sweating and puffing up a storm. A girl in purple Coke-bottle glasses flaps a *Seventeen* magazine like it's a fan; a pony-tailed Jennifer Connelly makes eyes at me from the cover.

Behind her, a kid with orange hair crosses his arms and blows exasperated bubbles with his Big League Chew.

The counselor holds up a pink slip. "Bacon. You're in Eagle Den. It's across the bridge at the far end of the lake. Don't fall in."

I snatch the paper from her and hustle away.

"Hey, Bacon, wait up, man!"

I turn and face Mr. Metallica. Cody. He stops to catch his breath and holds up a finger. "I'm in—I'm in Eagle Den, too. Looks like we're bunkmates. Where you from?"

"St. Paul," I mutter. "You?"

"Minneapolis. Hey, we're neighbors. You new here? I don't remember you from last year."

"Yeah. First time."

"I lost forty pounds last summer," Cody says. "Mom was pretty impressed, but"—he makes a ribbon of fat with his stomach and shakes it—"I gained it right back. Fuckin' Big Macs, man. They get me every time." He eyes me. "So, what's your story?"

I'm fat. End of story. "My parents made me come."

"Don't be so glum, chum," Cody says. "It ain't half-bad here. I mean, the food sucks and all, but the rest of it's okay. And did you see Cindi back there? *Dayum*, she's hot, right?" He elbows me and winks. "*Right?*"

I can't argue that.

"She's the best part of this place. Sometimes, she tans on the dock in this little yellow bikini. *Gawd.* I brought some binoculars this year. I want to get a better view."

It's all sorts of wrong, but I already know I'll be joining him.

"The worst part is the mornings," he continues. "Waking up at the ass crack of dawn for all the exercise. It *suucccks*. Especially the burpees. Ugh. But they mostly leave us alone in the afternoon. There's a group of us that play Dungeons and Dragons if you want in."

Now *that* gets me excited, but I try to play it cool. Girls like Cindi aren't exactly into the D&D type. "Oh, yeah?"

He nods. "Yup. C'mon. I'll show you our place."

"Our place" is a shithole. It's cramped and drafty with cracks in the log walls large enough to see through and floors covered in so much grime that they might as well be dirt. Four twin-sized beds with green vinyl mattresses run the length of the room. I pick one near the back and toss my suitcase on it. I'm surprised. I'd been expecting bunks, but it makes sense. Bunk beds at fat camp are probably a major liability. A few loose screws and you're toast.

The screen door thwacks open to a Black kid in a blue denim jacket and a white kid with curls so thick, I wonder if they're home to a bird or two. The white kid drops his bag and issues Cody a mock salute.

"Hey, hey, it's the Codester!"

"Yo, Erik! Looks like we're bunking up again!"

Cody stomps over and gives him a series of high fives with lots of finger snaps and fist bumps—clearly something they worked out last summer.

"Yup," the Black kid—Erik—replies. He jerks a thumb my way. "Who's the new guy?"

"Yeah, right. Erik and Matt, meet Bobby."

I know it's coming before he says it.

"Bobby *Bacon*."

I feel my cheeks flare up again. I want to punch him.

"No way? Serious?" Erik asks, his eyes bugging out. "Your name's Bacon?"

I exhale and struggle not to roll my eyes. "Yep."

"Dude, righteous! Bacon. I love it. Best name ever. I'm Erik." He strides over and shakes my hand. My palm comes away dripping with his sweat. He slaps the white kid on the back. "And this is Matt."

Matt raises a hand and looks like he's about to say something when the door bangs open again. This time, it's a guy who looks just like Johnny Lawrence from *The Karate Kid*, but prettier, with biceps the size of grapefruits and spiked hair so peroxide-bleached that it glows. A lanyard sways from his neck: *Tanner Holden, Camp Director.*

Even his name rocks. I hate him instantly.

"Bag check, maggots! Unzip 'em and rip 'em," he says. "And I better not find a single goddamn candy bar anywhere. No care packages or sweet treats from your mommies, or you're all doing laps tonight."

He destroys Cody's bag first. Cody shoots me a quick eye roll as his clothes spray out like fireworks, his toiletries clattering atop the pile. Tanner moves to Erik's suitcase next and cocks his head at something—a *Playboy* which he grabs and holds up. It's the Victoria Sellers issue. She leers from the cover with a red-gloved finger resting playfully on her lower lip. I gag. For some reason, she reminds me of my older sister Sally playing dress-up.

"Well, well, well, at least someone in here likes pussy," Tanner says, running a hand through his spiked hair. I expect it to come away bleeding. He glances at Erik, then throws a fake punch. Erik flinches and sits down hard on his bed. Tanner howls with laughter and shakes his head. "*Psych.* I'm just fuckin' with you, man. Dinner's in ten. Be there or be square." He glares at the rest of us. "All of you." With that, he's gone, barging back outside.

Erik shoots him the bird. "*That* asshole is the camp director? What happened to Mr. Wilson?"

"Dunno," Matt replies with a shrug. "But I've never seen that guy before."

"Yeah, me neither," Cody adds. "Now that you mention it, I think the only counselor I recognize from last year is Cindi."

"Cindi." Erik says with a sigh. "Such a babe. Think she's dating anyone?"

"Probably that muscle-head jerk," Matt replies. "Chicks dig the assholes."

"Forget him," Cody says, lurching for the door. "Let's go get some grub." He glances at me. "Bacon, be prepared. The food here stinks."

The *mess hall* stinks. Literally. It smells like wet cabbage mixed with dog food.

I grab a tray with food compartments stamped in it and set it in front of a lady in a hairnet ladling out spoonfuls of some formless brown mass. Her name tag reads *Mrs. Yoshika*. She regards me with all the enthusiasm of a Walmart door greeter as she plops a scoop on my tray. I stare at it with my stomach in a twist.

"Ey, you want second scoop?" she asks with a wink.

"Huh?"

"Okay. I give you one more." Before I can escape, she slaps another formless serving down. It looks like liquified meatloaf.

"What *is* this stuff?" I ask. There's nothing else—no bread or salad. Nothing. I'm not about to eat this crap.

She waves a gloved hand at me. "Go. Go."

"You better do what she says, man," Cody whispers, nudging me along. "She'll cut you."

We find a table near the back that's already jammed with campers. I wedge myself in next to a girl with mousy red hair and a face bleeding freckles. She gives me a glittery smile, her braces flashing. "Hi. I'm Lexi. What cabin are you in?"

"Hey. Bobby. I'm—" The lights go out before I can finish the sentence.

A deep rumble fills the room: a bass guitar thumping out the notes to "Another One Bites the Dust." Freddie Mercury tears in, and the lights snap on again. Tanner stands at the front of the room wearing mirror-lens aviators, one hand clutching a gleaming microphone over his head, his fist pumping with the beat. Counselors fan away on either side of him, the girls clad in a rainbow of neon spandex leggings. Purple. Pink. Baby blue. I stare, slack-jawed. They look like they belong in a Coppertone commercial.

"Holy shit," Cody whispers to my right. "So many babes."

The music cuts off. "Welcome, campers!" Tanner blares into the microphone. "This year's gonna be a little different." He grabs a tray from a boy tucking into his pile of slop with gusto and tosses it across the room like a frisbee. "Who actually wants to eat this crap?"

"Not me. This food sucks!" a boy shouts from somewhere behind me. Heads nod in agreement.

"What are you waiting for, then? Trash this shit!"

Cody stands first, grabs his tray, and slumps over to the garbage can. He shrugs and tosses it in. *Thunk.*

More kids follow. *Thunk. Thunk.*

We move, trays scraping off the tables, kids cheering and shouting in a mad race to the garbage cans. Mrs. Yoshika scuttles from behind the serving line, waving her hands and shaking her head furiously. A beefy counselor loops an arm around her shoulder and escorts her to the kitchen.

Thunk. Thunk. Thunk.

"Now, *that's* what I'm talking about!" Tanner cries.

The music clicks on, Freddie Mercury back at it. More counselors burst through the kitchen doors carrying trays layered in hamburgers and hotdogs and bright green bags of Lay's potato chips. My stomach growls.

"It's all yours," Tanner says. "As much as you can handle! Eat up!"

Kids cheer and whoop, looking at each other with stunned expressions that mirror the one twisting over my face. High fives are in no short supply. Erik tucks into a hamburger across from me, his fist full of fries. "This is bitchin'," he sputters, spraying food my way. He eyes my hotdog. "You gonna eat that?"

I dig in before he can grab it. I gorge myself. The meat is a little tough, but it's ten times better than the garbage Mrs. Yoshika tried to serve us. I mop up the burger grease with the fries and have seconds. The counselors keep bringing more out, the girls winking as they pile our plates high.

Dessert follows in the form of ice-cream sundaes and chocolate cake layered in cream cheese frosting. Trays of cookies are delivered to each table. Mouths grow muddy with crumbs all around me.

I stop mid-bite. It doesn't make sense. The Camp Klehani flier advertised portion control and a well-balanced diet. This is anything *but* well-balanced. This is madness. But I'm not about to complain.

Tanner saunters over and crouches down next to Erik. He has his aviators off. Gray eyes. Strange. For some reason, I'd expected blue. They chat for a bit, Tanner ragging Erik good-naturedly about his *Playboy* again while jerking his hand up and down before thumbing his nose.

"You party, man?"

Erik goes blank-faced, a fat kid invited to the weekend kegger by the star quarterback. "I, uh—yeah. Yeah, for sure, dude. Totally."

Tanner leans close and says something in a hushed tone. Movement ripples across his cheek. It looks like an earthworm burrowing through dirt. I blink and rub my eyes. When I look back, he's dancing his way to another table.

Erik catches my gaze and pops an eyebrow. "Holy shit, did you see that, bro?"

"Yeah...what did he say?"

"I, um...I'm not supposed to tell."

"C'mon, man," I prod. "Spill it."

"Well..." he leans across the table and cups a hand to his mouth in a barely concealed whisper. "Tanner wants me to stay. After all this, you know?" He glances from side to side like someone is listening. No one is. "He said I might score with one of these counselor chicks if I play it cool. He told me the brunette over there thinks I'm cute. Can you believe that?"

I can't. I can barely speak, I'm so jealous.

Dinner sputters out slowly from there. Kids filter outside in packs. Cody, Matt, and I follow. Erik is already planted at Tanner's table with a few other lucky campers, Lexi included. She notices me looking and flutters a wave as we tumble into the cool evening air.

"Dude, was that not *insane?*" Cody says. "Tell me that's not the craziest shit you've ever seen. I was wrong about Tanner. The guy rocks!"

Matt gives a hard nod, his curls bouncing. "Totally. So much better than Mr. Wilson's crew."

"Yeah, that guy never stopped with his stupid slogans." Cody throws up some air quotes. "'Give your body the proper nutrients and it will do the rest.' 'Eat well to live well.' 'Progress, not perfection.' Blah, blah, blah. Suck my dick." He says it in a high-pitched tone I take as a poor imitation of Mr. Wilson. Apparently, it's hilarious, because they both double over with laughter.

When Cody comes up for air, it's with an, "Oh, shit."

"What?" I ask.

"We forgot Erik."

Tanner's invitation rings hot in my head. *You like to party?* I wave Cody off. "Tanner invited him to hang out." *And do some coke.* I'm pretty sure I remember the nose-tap thing from an episode of *Miami Vice*. I'm also pretty sure Mom wouldn't be too thrilled to know about the extracurriculars going on here at Camp Klehani.

Matt cocks a hip to the side and crosses his arms. "What? No frickin' way. Erik? What'd he do that was so special?"

"No clue. I heard Tanner invite him, though. I think the *Playboy* got him in."

"No fair," Matt whines. "My Dad has a stack of *Penthouse* in his closet. If I'd known, I woulda swiped a few."

Cody claps him on the back and burps, then spouts off a terrible British accent: "Alas, my good man, let Sir Erik haveth his time in the sun, for ours soon shall be nigh!"

"Huh?" Matt asks.

"I said, forget him. We got us some D&D to play."

The prospect cheers me up significantly. We go back to the cabin and play until two a.m.

I don't think about Erik once.

We lurch from the cabin the next morning around ten, our eyes grainy with sleep. A piss-yellow sun hangs overhead, centered in a cloudless sky.

"I don't get it," Cody mutters. "No stupid bugle? They always have us up by seven at the latest for the morning stretch. I'm starved."

Matt yawns. "Me, too."

"They have all kinds of food out in the mess hall." It's a girl's voice, a hefty brunette in a pink and purple bathing suit with a towel clutched in her hand. "Everyone's heading up to the lake if you guys wanna come after you eat."

"What about fitness?" Matt asks, digging something from his ear.

"Cancelled."

"Rad!" His face buckles. "Wait...why?"

"Dunno. But I like it. See ya." She waves and trots off, bouncing on the balls of her feet.

I glance back into the cabin at Erik's bed, his bag still tipped on its side, vomiting a pile of clothes over the bare mattress. A lot of denim. His Walkman.

"Did anyone see Erik come back last night?" I ask.

Cody shakes his head.

"He's probably eating already," Matt replies, slapping his stomach. "I say we go join him."

Breakfast is another ridiculous spread of doughnuts, breakfast burritos, eggs, bacon, toast, and pancakes, which we devour before heading back to the lake. We spend the day staring at Cindi and the other goddess counselors. They're sprawled out in a field of golden skin on the dock, some with their tops unfastened. They mist each other with water bottles. They lotion each other's backs. Madonna chimes "Like a Virgin" from a boombox.

I feel like I'm watching soft-core porn; I want to run into the woods and masturbate. It's ridiculous.

Sometime around mid-afternoon, I think of Erik again. Cody has his shirt off, his man boobs glistening pink with an early sunburn. Matt's perched on a rock with his jeans rolled up over a pair of chalk-white thighs.

"Guys," I say, "don't you think we should do something about Erik? Shouldn't he be back by now?"

Cody shrugs. "He's probably at the cabin sleeping it off. Sex takes a lot of work."

"Like you would know," Matt says.

"Dude, I've totally had sex."

"With who?" Matt asks. "Your hand?"

I laugh. Cody glares at me.

"You think he *actually* scored?" Matt asks.

Cody picks at something in his teeth. "Probably."

I snap my fingers at them. "Hey, guys, forget about all that shit for a minute. What's going on here? Isn't this all a little weird? All this food? Everyone just doing whatever they want all day?"

Cody blows a raspberry with his lips. "Dude, relax. It's frickin' *awesome* is what it is. Matt, tell Bacon to stop getting his panties in a bunch."

Matt slaps at a mosquito and holds it up, squishing it between his thumb and forefinger. "Chillax, Bacon. It's not every day you get to—"

"My dudes!"

I jerk back toward Tanner and two other counselors hovering over us with their shirts off, their abs rippling like they've just stepped off a Gold's Gym billboard.

"Who here knows how to party?" Tanner asks before I can mention Erik.

Matt's hand shoots up. "Me! Me! I know how to party."

Tanner smirks. "Hmm, I don't know, man." He looks at the other guys. "You think this kid can party? He doesn't look like he knows how to party."

The counselor closest to him massages his lips. "Yeah, I dunno…" He glances at the other counselor, a guy with olive skin and a square jaw. "What do you think, Dave?"

"I say we give the kid a shot," Dave replies. "What can it hurt?" A tremor runs through his face as he says it. More rippling worms. It happens so fast, I wonder if I've imagined it.

Tanner shoots Matt a Polaroid grin and claps his hands together. "Okay, kid, you're in. I'll stop by your cabin after dinner. You better bring your A-game, though. You *do not* want to disappoint the babes. Especially not Cindi."

Matt nods so hard, I think his head will pop off.

Cody's voice squeaks to life as they turn to leave. "W-wait, guys. Guys. Me, too. I know how to party."

Tanner glances back without stopping. "Sorry, bro. Not tonight. You'll get your chance, though...*if* you play your cards right."

There's something about the way he says it that I don't like. It sounds more like a threat than a promise.

Matt's eyebrows pop so high, I'm worried they'll leap off his face. "Oh, my god. Oh, my god. I need to shower. I need—oh shit, you guys have any condoms? I think I might need a condom. I totally forgot to bring one."

"You suck, man," Cody says with a groan.

I don't hear a word. I'm too busy watching Tanner and his bros muscle their way down the shoreline. One thought picks at me the rest of the day and through dinner:

This is all too easy.

Tanner swings by around eight o'clock, wearing a black leather bomber jacket and his mirrored aviators. Tonight, he looks more like Ice Man from *Top Gun* than Johnny Lawrence. He takes a swig from the red Solo cup in his hand and clicks a piece of ice against his teeth. When he raises his glasses, I wither beneath his gravel-colored gaze. "Hey, Pudge. Where's the kid? He ready?"

"Um, yeah, he's—"

Matt bursts from the bathroom in a cloud of cologne. Brut. "I'm right here! Just, ah, you know, getting my game face on." He's in full-on party mode in a pair of frayed, acid-wash jeans and a purple track-suit top stamped in yellow and pink triangles. A black sweatband strangles his forehead, his hair curling over it like it's been freshly permed. He spreads his arms wide and wiggles his fingers. "Whaddya think? This work?"

"Sure, kid, whatever," Tanner says, indifferent. "The babes will love it. Now, let's go."

Cody blows an annoyed breath from his bed and rolls onto his side.

Matt eases past me with a dopey smile and a fist bump, mouthing a quick, *Oh, my god.* They're halfway out the door before I stop them.

"Hey, Tanner!"

He groans to a stop. "You're killing me, Pudge. What?"

"Have you seen Erik?"

"Who?"

"The kid you took to"—I flash a set of air quotes—"party last night? He never came back."

"Ohhh, that kid. Right. He partied too hard. His parents came by and took him home. Guess he couldn't handle it." He makes a gun with his hand and cocks his thumb. Fires it at me. "Now, be a good little camper and go to bed."

He flings an arm around Matt, and they march off, his voice echoing through my skull.

His parents came by? No way. Erik told me they live seven hours away in some bumfuck town in Iowa. The itch hits again, the feeling that this place is a bunch of—

"Bullshit!"

I jerk back. Cody stands a foot away, tugging on his jacket and reeking of hair gel. "I'm crashing the party, man. No way is Matt cooler than us, Bacon. No effing way, bro. He doesn't even work out." He surges by me and stops, glancing back. His acne scars glow beneath the dim cabin light. "You coming, or what?"

We catch up with them before they hit the forest. The moon hangs above us in full, spotlight-white. Not a cloud in the sky.

Tanner still has his arm wrapped around Matt, but not in a fun, *hey-let's-go-get-you-wasted* kind of way. No, this is more of a *you-try-to-run-and-I'll-snap-your-neck* grip, not that Matt seems to mind. He bops right along next to Tanner, oblivious. Probably thinking about which girl he's about to bang.

Except there aren't any girls. Only a dark wall of pine trees.

We hustle after them up a rocky trail winding through the ponderosa. Trees hem us in on both sides like giant slivers of bone, the branches filtering out the stars. We move as quietly as two fat kids can, which is not at all, but we're silent enough that Tanner only stops once, glancing back over his shoulder when Cody kicks a stone loose. We duck behind a jagged clump of granite before he's able to spot us, and I want to tell Cody we should go back, that what we're doing is crazy. I can tell he wants to say the same, but neither of us wants to bitch out first. Teenage boy code.

My legs burn as we wind deeper into the woods, my quads trembling. I feel like I'm on a StairMaster. We hear the crackle of the bonfire before we see it, pine boughs flickering with a dusty orange light that makes me think of every B-horror movie I've ever seen. The dumb kids walking straight toward the monster. I jerk Cody back behind some underbrush when we hit the ridgeline.

"What the hell, man?" he hisses, nearly tripping.

I point. "*Look.*"

A fire the size of a small shed crackles downslope in a low bowl of earth. Campers and counselors are circled around the blaze, the female counselors wearing lace-white dresses with flower crowns planted atop their heads. It's not exactly party gear, but I have to admit they look pretty damn hot. Everyone has beers in hand, and a couple of campers are passing a joint. One of them, a Chinese kid I recognize from the first day in the cafeteria, takes a hit and coughs so hard that I think he'll spit out a lung.

"Pfft. What a rookie," Cody whispers.

Matt and Tanner head toward a cooler and snag a couple of beers. Tanner cracks his and takes the entire thing down in one long pull. His burp rings through the trees like a grizzly's roar.

"Screw this," Cody says. "I'm gonna join them." He starts forward, and I jerk him back. "Man, Bacon, if you don't let go of me right now…"

"Shut up," I hiss, thrusting a finger. "Look."

He follows my gaze and his nose creases. "What the hell?"

The female counselors have formed a circle around the campers. Tanner eases behind one of them, a blonde with watermelon boobs, and unzips her dress. Normally, it would be the stuff of wet dreams, but the way this girl is moving—her limbs snapping back and forth, her jaw clicking open and shut so hard that her breasts are bouncing—is disturbing. The other male counselors do the same, each of them sliding behind a female counselor to remove her dress. The campers stare at them with their faces glazed in a collection of *what-the-fuck* looks.

Tanner tips his chin toward the moon and howls.

The sound is unlike anything I've ever heard—a piercing, inhuman shriek. Then, he does something that sends a slug of acid racing up my throat.

He unzips his girl's *skin.*

He starts beneath her hairline, at the nape of her neck, and pulls.

And pulls, and pulls...

Down to her ankles.

What slides out is straight from hell. A glistening black tangle of arms and legs with two-inch teeth shredded to the gums, planted beneath four pearl-white, luminescent eyes. Serrated shards of bone extend from its elbows and knees. And it isn't alone. All of the counselors are ripping off their clothes, their *skins*. An army of black-sludge bodies wriggle free, creatures with slick flesh studded in sharp splinters of bone.

"Holy fuck," Cody whispers.

The cafeteria kid is the first to scream. I'm pretty sure he pisses his pants as they swarm him. It's like watching a bleating cow tossed into a boiling mass of piranha. They go after his face first, their teeth shredding him. Slicing.

The other campers scatter.

Matt makes it to the treeline before one of the things hooks his ankle and drags him back. He screams like a girl as it tears into his calf.

Cody gags. Something hot splashes off his shoes.

"What are you two doing up here?"

My heart explodes. I jerk around to glimpse a dark figure and nearly black out before I recognize the voice. Cindi. I half-expect her to rip off her skin like the others before Cody's words ring through my head: *"She's the only one I recognize from last year."*

"What's all this noi—"

Cody clamps a hand over her mouth. "*Shhhh.*"

Her eyes bulge as she claws at his wrist.

"We-we gotta go. They're *eating* them," Cody hisses.

Cindi stiffens, and Cody slowly lifts his hand.

She smiles. "I know."

Black talons explode from the tips of her fingers. She sinks them into Cody's forearm and goes for his neck with her teeth. She comes away with a bloody chunk of his throat in her mouth.

I run.

Branches rip at my face, my arms. Rocks carve into my knees. Piles of deadfall slash at my shins. Adrenaline spurts through my veins and turns my legs to rubber. I stumble and fight through tangles of bracken—blind, save for the moonlight cutting across the forest floor. Cindi tears through the brush after me…

…and shrieks.

The other counselors answer her call with their own screams. Quick, frantic bursts like gunshots. Metal on metal.

I know what that means. They're hunting.

I angle from the path and leap over a rotten log, my landing awkward and heavy. A hot bolt of pain rips through my ankle. The ground steepens, and everything picks up speed. I'm not running, really; I'm being jerked downhill by gravity, my feet somehow keeping up, but only barely. I don't turn.

Don't look back.

I know what I'll see.

Her joints click behind me, her limbs spearing the earth like a set of steel pistons, drawing closer. I feel her hot, rancid breath on my neck, her teeth grazing my skin.

I fall.

Rolling. Bashing off rocks and scree, the forest popping in and out in a series of flashes. Black. White. Black. White. Black.

My head cracks against a boulder, and my vision supernovas for a second before I lurch into dead air.

I hit water. *Smack!*

My breath explodes, hanging above me in a thousand silver bubbles. I flop against the current.

The river. I'm in the river. The thought floats up as if from a dream. *Swim, you dumbass!*

I do, flapping and stroking, my clothes so water-logged that they drag me under. I slam into a pile of rocks and choke for air, gulping water instead. My vision blackens and curls at the edges. Winks out.

Then, there's air in my throat, beautiful air, and the rapids are slowing, dragging me toward the riverbank.

When my fingers hit mud, I almost cry out. I pull myself onto the bank and cough a lungful of river from my lungs. Upstream, a shriek carves through the trees. Another. I see the branches swaying, black forms leaping through the woods.

Broken and bleeding, I scramble beneath a hollow shelf of earth and wedge myself behind a dense curtain of roots. My breath comes fast, my ankle throbbing in time with my racing heart.

I'm pretty sure I've broken a few ribs, and my forehead burns like crazy, blood leeching dark and sticky into my eyes. I barely have time to register its heat before I hear them.

They're horrifyingly fast. Their voices, if you can call them that, gutter and pop around me. Think of a train scraping over the tracks with the heat brakes screeching, only worse. *So* much worse.

One of them stalks closer, its teeth chattering—*click, click, click.* It snorts in a lurching, wet breath before blowing it out in a hiss. Silence. Air slides slow into a wet pair of nostrils as talons curl over the bank and set loose a shivering cloud of dust.

No, no, no, no, no...

I slap a hand to my mouth and bite the web of flesh between my forefinger and thumb until I taste copper. An oil-black head appears. A sliver of milk-pale eyes.

A shrill cry rises in the distance. The thing above me jerks skyward and answers, and then it's gone.

My bladder empties.

I lay there the entire night and listen to them shriek. Spiders flurry over my skin. Insects burrow into my hair. I let them. I don't move a fucking muscle. At some point—I don't know whether from injury, exhaustion, or both—I succumb to sleep. When I wake up, I'm covered in dew, the sun sparkling through the trees in a pink blush.

Matt's scream rips through my head, and I'm back to listening for the creatures, my entire body stiff, my heart in a full-on thunder. I think of Cody's face, relive the panic flooding his eyes a second before Cindi smiled and tore out his throat.

I shudder and listen. Listen and shudder.

For hours.

Somewhere around mid-morning, I pull myself from my hiding place and limp downriver until I hit the highway, where I collapse on the shoulder beneath an ancient white pine. Half an hour passes before anyone stops. I'm busy rubbing my freezing fingers back to life when I spot the semi rumbling around the corner—a blue Peterbilt with an extended cab. It screeches to a halt, and the door kicks open to a face that's all beard and sunglasses beneath a John Deere ball cap pulled low.

"Need a lift, kid?"

I stare at him and consider running. He looks normal enough, but then again, so did Tanner and Cindi. It doesn't matter. Even if I wanted to, I wouldn't make it another step. I nod and climb aboard. My arms are so bruised, it hurts to buckle my seatbelt.

"Jesus, what happened to you, son?" he asks through a mouthful of chew.

"The police...get me to the police."

"Looks more like I should take you to a hospital."

I fight back tears. "No. The cops. I…I need the cops. There were these things in the forest… Please. The police."

"Whatever you need, boss. There's a station in Spring Junction. It's just up the road. I'll drop you there." He pops the air brakes, and we're off. We ride in silence. A picture of a woman, tan as a leather bag, sways from the rearview mirror. An army of bobbleheads clutter the dash and nod me to sleep.

When my eyes drift open again, it's to a pounding headache and the back of my neck stinging like someone's drenched it in battery acid. I finger it with a hiss and remember Cindi's teeth snapping as I fell into the river.

Jesus, she fucking bit me.

"You okay, kid?" the man asks, side-eyeing me through his glasses.

"I think so. Where are we?"

"Getting close now. Station's right up the road."

The gravel road, I realize as a set of cheerfully stenciled letters come into view: *Welcome to Camp Klehani!*

I leap for the door. The handle doesn't budge.

The man laughs and raises his sunglasses. His eyes shine the same wet concrete color as Tanner's. Because it *is* Tanner, I realize, too late. Tanner wearing a new suit of flesh, and staring at me like I'm the Sunday morning eggs and bacon breakfast special.

"Don't worry, Pudge," he says. "We ain't gonna eat'cha the way we did the others. Isn't that right, Cindi?"

I sense her rising behind me. Feel a splash of her hot, musty breath spill past my cheeks. A cold metal finger slides across the back of my neck where she bit me. "Noooo," she says. "Noooo."

Tanner slaps a hand on my knee and squeezes, his teeth dripping with tobacco juice. "You see, kid? You're safe. You wouldn't taste any good." His smile broadens, and he glances back to the road. "Not now that you're one of us."

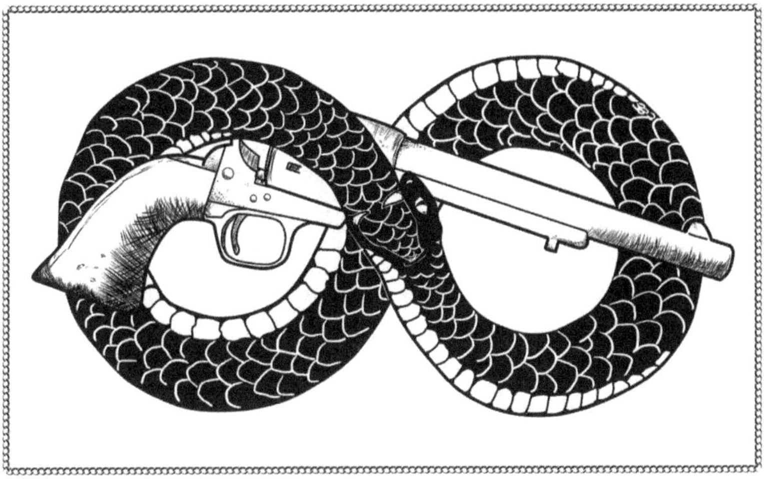

STAY OUT OF THE SWAMP, JASPER DOUCET

1886

The Three Goats Tavern stank of brine and smoke, ill-lit with candles that painted the windowsills in rainbows of wax. An accordion sang from the corner. Men whose beards were stitched with scars sat crowded around thick slabs of oak, concerning themselves with the business of getting drunk.

Jasper "Two-Gun" Doucet watched them from the bar. They were a ghastly lot packed with swindlers and pickpockets, outlaws like him who'd long fled the cinch of a hangman's noose out west. One of them, a giant with an eyepatch, emptied his mug, attempted to stand, and promptly fell to the floor amidst a great roar of laughter.

Jasper smiled. It was good to be home.

He drained his whiskey and nodded for Dylan to do the same.

His nephew made no move for the tumbler. "I ain't of age, Uncle Jasper. And Ma wouldn't of approved."

Jasper chuckled and waved at the bartender for another. "Shit, kid, your ma's dead. Lord knows I loved my sister, but that woman could have lived a little more. Now, raise your damn glass so I can toast her proper."

That did the trick. Dylan lifted the tumbler and Jasper clinked it. "To Lisette. A finer woman, Louisiana has never known."

"To Ma," Dylan echoed with a wince.

They emptied their glasses, and Dylan coughed as he slammed his back in its sweat ring. "How do you..." He cleared his throat. "How do you drink this stuff?"

Jasper clapped him on the back. "Takes practice, young Mr. Broussard. Lots of practice."

"Can we leave?" Dylan asked. "I ain't feelin' so hot."

Jasper grinned. "Soon as we get us some grub."

"You should listen to him."

The voice came from their right, and Jasper swiveled on his stool to find a woman appraising him with two clouded eyes, her irises ringed in white. Matted ropes of hair framed a face that was as black as the midnight sky, cracked from years of salt and sun. Rings engraved with strange symbols cluttered her fingers, and she had a smile that was mostly silver.

Jasper's blood ran cold. He knew the type—a *sorcière*, a voodoo witch.

"Where's the pisser, Uncle Jasper?" Dylan asked. "I gotta pee something fierce."

Jasper ignored him and focused on the woman. "Pardon?"

"I said you two should git," she replied. "Now, before he comes."

Jasper's brow knit together. "Who?"

"Him."

The woman looked away then, past the rows of glittering liquor bottles and toward a broad mirror mounted behind the bar. And though she had the eyes of a blind woman, they seemed to focus on something—a reflection crystallizing in the glass, growing clearer.

An old man stumbled through the saloon doors, cloaked in a mud-spattered, double-breasted duster. A ragged scar carved down his face and burrowed beneath a ramshackle beard. His hair was greased with sweat, and he had eyes that were wild and confused as they bounced over the room in search of something.

Jasper met his gaze in the mirror. No, not something. Some*one*.

Him.

Jasper spun around as Dylan lurched to his feet and stumbled directly into Jasper's view of the man.

"I really gotta pee, Uncle—"

The gunshot rang out an instant before the insides of Dylan's skull painted Jasper's forehead in a warm red mist. Jasper blinked and reached for the .45 Schofield revolver strapped to his hip. A look of recognition hung on the old man's face, one of shock, but it wasn't enough to keep Jasper's finger from the trigger.

The bullet took the man in his gut and sent him spinning back through the doors and into the steaming night.

With a cry, Jasper dropped to the floor and pulled Dylan's ruined head into his lap. He saw his sister then, clear as day, Lisette lying upon her death bed with her desiccated skin wrapped around the sharp angles of her face, her eyes swimming with fever.

"Promise me you'll keep him safe, Jasper. Swear it on your life."

"On my life, Lizzy. I swear."

A promise he'd now turned to piss.

"No, no, no," he muttered as he thumbed the hole in Dylan's forehead. The hole meant for him.

Two bowls of gumbo shattered on the bar behind him. "*Dieu nous garde!* Who done this?"

Jasper pulled Dylan's eyelids closed and stood. The bartender appraised him with a look of blank horror, his gaze coming to rest on the bits of brain matter now clumped in Jasper's beard. Jasper reached into his coat pocket and slapped two bits of silver onto the scarred wood. "See to my nephew's body, and there'll be more where this came from. Don't, and I'll come for you next."

The man crossed himself and nodded.

Jasper strode for the door.

"Stay out of the swamp, Jasper Doucet!" the witch called after him. "You would be wise to remember revenge burns in a circle."

How the woman knew his name, Jasper didn't know…or care.

He had a man to kill.

Outside, the night air hung thick as a sponge, bathing his skin in moisture as he marched across Clément Square toward a group of men staring into a wall of cypress. Jasper seized the lapels of the tallest, though not nearly as tall as him, and gave them a firm shake.

"Where'd he go?"

"Who?" The man's eyes were red, riddled with veins, and his breath stank of rum.

"The vagrant," Jasper growled.

The man blinked and raised a scabbed finger toward the trees. "He gone into the swamp, *monsieur*. He left you a trail."

Jasper followed the man's gaze toward two dark coins of blood pooled on the cobblestone. Whoever this coward was, Jasper's bullet had caught him square.

He wouldn't get far.

Jasper inhaled the rich, wet scent of the bayou. The smell of sulfur and salt was as much a part of him as the oxygen that filled his lungs and reddened his blood. He'd spent his youth not far from here, near Natchitoches, trawling for bass and crawfish with his younger brother Carson. Their father—a man of few smiles and even fewer words—had regaled them with the same warning every time they'd launched the pirogue.

"Remember, mes garçons, *everything in the swamp wants to kill you, and if you ever think it don't, you're dead already."*

The words rang true enough. Men didn't scare Jasper half as much as a copperhead coiled in the grass, or a black widow waiting to fall on his neck from the branches of a gum tree. He'd trapped and skinned gators twice the length of a horse who could've twisted his arm clean from its socket in a single bite. He had a man to kill, yes, but he'd need to move with care, or it would be him who wound up dead instead of his quarry.

The marsh came to life around him as he followed the man's tracks. Cicadas pulsed and buzzed from high atop the dense canopy of leaves. Bullfrogs sang to one another in rolling croaks, their songs pierced at times by the caterwauling shriek of a barred owl in hunt of voles. A three-quarter moon hung overhead, painting the cypress trees in chalky white light. Ribbons of Spanish moss dripped from their skeletal branches, giving them the appearance of corpse arms strung in tattered robes.

Jasper moved at a steady clip, and it wasn't long before he spotted the bastard standing doubled-over near a row of mangroves. He raised a blood-stained hand as Jasper neared, his palm shining black against the pale wash of moonlight. "Go back…you—" A cough boiled in his lungs, and he spat to the side. "You have to go back."

"Tell me your name," Jasper growled, this time unholstering his Colt single action, "and I'll make it quick. Don't, and I'll take my time."

The man barked out a ragged laugh. "You're a damn fool if you don't know who I am."

Before he could respond, there came the crack of a twig from behind Jasper, followed by a voice steeped in smoke.

"Well, well, if it ain't Two-Gun Doucet."

Jasper spun around to a man with a pitted face and a gut that strained the buttons of his dress shirt. "Remember me?"

Jasper felt the ground pitch beneath his feet.

He did. John Dunbar—a mean sonuvabitch with breath that could strip varnish. He'd come to collect the bounty on Jasper's head a month before Lisette had sent word she'd taken ill. He'd ambushed Jasper near Bandera, and Jasper had barely managed to shoot him dead beneath a yellow-piss sun.

"I missed my daughter's wedding 'cause of you," John Dunbar continued. "Figure I owe you for that."

He went for his gun.

Jasper sent a bullet into the fat man's heart before he reached his pistol grip and put a second through his skull for good measure.

John Dunbar toppled in slow motion, bursting into a cloud of buzzing insects the second he hit the slop. Swarms of yellowjackets and biting flies sent Jasper scrambling backward until he lost his footing and sat down hard in the muck.

His breath came in quick snatches. Mosquitoes sang in his ears.

To kill a man twice was against the natural order of things. It made no sense. He wondered, briefly, if he'd lost his mind.

After a time, he remembered the old man and twisted around with his guns drawn, but all that greeted him were trees and starlight. A seed of doubt tore at his gut. The old coot could have shot him. Easily. Could have plugged him in the back of the head and put an end to all this. But he hadn't.

He'd fled again instead. *Why?*

Jasper regained his footing and canvased the bog until he spotted a pair of boot tracks winding away down a boar trail that skirted a flat plane of water. Flowers dotted its surface—clumps of tiger lotus and spider lilies in full bloom, their petals uncurling across the marsh in a thousand pale white fountains.

He stared at them and thought again of the old man. Jasper had a way with faces—near-photographic—and something about the bastard tickled his brain. The fact that he couldn't place what was worrisome. Not to mention the way he'd eyed Jasper, had told him to go back…

It all seemed *off*.

But it didn't change the fact he'd killed Dylan, and Jasper would be damned if he'd let the cocksucker live to see another sunrise.

Thick tendrils of fog filled the air, turning the garlands of Spanish moss into shadows as he pressed deeper into the swamp. The croak of a heron carried through the mist, followed by the low, thrumming chorus of bullfrogs. An hour passed, or two—Jasper couldn't tell anymore—before he spotted something near a copse of white oak that gave him pause. It was a shape he recognized—a smooth band of polished wood peppered in bronze lettering.

Wells Fargo & Company.

Jasper knew the coach because he'd robbed it; he and the two men propped against it. The Flores brothers.

Jasper rubbed his eyes, certain he was hallucinating.

He wasn't.

There they stood, Mateo and Lucas, staring right back at him as if he hadn't punched their tickets to hell a year earlier. They'd been of the filthy sort, slow to reason and quick to anger—especially when it came to their women, whom they'd treated worse than their dogs. Jasper had sworn he'd kill them as soon as the chance arose, and kill them he had, with a bullet each from the Colt and the Schofield. They'd fallen together, clutching their chests, and Jasper had pissed on their boots as they'd died.

The corpse of Mateo Flores uncrossed his arms and gave Jasper a wicked grin. His cheeks were pocked with holes, his neck stripped to the tendons. "Thought you'd rid yourself of us, did you, you murderin' sumbitch?"

Lucas Flores cocked his 1860 Henry, as good a shot with the rifle as any man Jasper had seen. Better, even. "Yellow bastard never gave us a chance. I'd say turnabout's fair play." He spat a rope of tobacco. "How 'bout you, brother?"

Mateo dipped his head. His nose was gone, his sinuses forming two black caves in the wan light. "I'd tend to agree."

Jasper sprang left as Mateo fired, a white trail of heat searing his abdomen. He returned the shot, taking Mateo high in the shoulder, and then sighted the barrel of his Colt on Lucas' forehead. It split like an egg beneath his bullet, but not before the 1860 Henry roared and sent a hot belt of lead through Jasper's ribs.

Black spots stung his vision. He tasted blood.

Mateo howled and rushed forward with a snarl, zigzagging through the sedge as Jasper fired, spraying bullets wide. The man was a blur: there one moment, gone the next, slipping in and out of the fog like a wraith. Then, he was up and charging Jasper with a dagger gleaming in his hand. Jasper raised the Colt, and the hammer clicked home empty. He switched to the Schofield, and the resulting blast took off the front quarter of Mateo's skull.

It wasn't enough. Mateo rammed into him, and they tumbled together, Mateo landing on Jasper's chest while driving the knife down toward his neck. Jasper swung his fist wide and managed to deflect the blade into his shoulder. Mateo laughed and twisted the knife deeper, sending bolts of lightning ripping down Jasper's arm until he cried out.

"Hurts, don't it, you back-stabbin' bastard?"

Jasper felt blindly for Mateo's hand and seized a finger, snapping it hard to the right. Mateo roared as it broke, flinching back far enough for Jasper to tear the knife from his shoulder and plunge it up through the man's scar-mottled chin. Gouts of blood pulsed from the wound and flooded into Jasper's eyes as well as his mouth. The fluid was foul beyond measure and stunk like a limb drenched in gangrene.

A low chuckle rose up Mateo's throat, his jaw working in place over the blade.

"Be…seein'…you again, Two-Gun. Be seein' you…real soon."

Chunks of flesh flaked from his cheeks as he spoke, along with swarms of maggots and balls of worms. Jasper gagged and rolled clear, slapping them from his face and chest—which, he discovered, no longer burned. He ran his fingers over his vest in search of the bullet hole from the Henry and found only untarnished leather. He prodded his gut. No hole there, either. Same with the wound carved into his shoulder by Mateo's knife.

Stay out of the swamp.

The witch's words came to him unbidden, the memory of those cold, marbled eyes sending a chill through his soul.

He should have listened. But that didn't change the fact he still had a man to kill.

With a deep breath, Jasper rose and continued down the boar trail, warier now as he followed the old man's tracks. Soon, he found himself standing before a dark tunnel of tupelo with branches that laced together overhead like the gnarled fingers of giants.

There came a whooshing through the leaves, the sound of twigs breaking, and, above him, a corpse snapped into place, dangling from the business end of a hangman's noose. Its head lolled to the side, revealing a face punctuated by two black eyes set above a slash of a mouth. From it tumbled a voice Jasper recognized—one rich with a southern drawl.

"Howdy, pardner. Long time."

His tongue went dry. Billy Johnson (but he went by Billy Blaze on account of his quickdraw speed) appraised him over the low creak of the rope. "Shoulda been you strung up here instead of me, ya know."

It was true. The bank job they'd pulled in Silver City had gone south, the sheriff and his men closing in on all sides. Jasper had had no choice but to take the moneybag and set Billy's horse loose when he'd mounted his. The lawmen had fallen upon Billy like a pack of jackals. His screams had chased Jasper clear to the edge of town.

"It ain't right what you done to me, Jasper," Billy croaked. "What you done to all of us. You'll burn for it soon enough, though. Devil's got a nice spot picked out for you right next to mine."

Billy's words skittered down Jasper's spine like a nest of fire ants as, ahead, more corpses shambled from the trees. Jasper knew them all: Jenny Pitkin, the whore he'd strangled after a night swilling rotgut in Arcola; Shane Marquez, the card shark whose neck he'd slit when the weasel had swindled his last dollar in Fort Gaines; the Thompson twins—Chester and Clay—who'd mocked him relentlessly when they'd discovered he couldn't read. Called him stupid.

Buck Ladner.

Maude McKinnon.

Dallas Webber.

All of them, everyone he'd ever killed, lining the trail in two neat rows.

But they weren't what Jasper's gaze came to rest on. He stared at the figure perched at the end of the tunnel, clad in a wool vest and a set of cotton trousers. A man framed in an oily patch of light. He drifted forward toward him, the dead watching Jasper pass with sightless eyes, their smoke-stained voices scraping across his eardrums and crawling over his skin.

"Damn you to hell, Jasper Doucet."

"Here comes the snake, Satan hisself."

"I'm comin' for you, Two-Gun. I'll kill you dead, you stupid shit."

Jasper ignored them all, his focus still on the man—no, he realized as he drew closer to the figure. It was a boy, one whose hair stood in a cowlick, and whose ears were spattered in a light dusting of freckles. Jasper's skin crimped with gooseflesh as he laid a hand upon the boy's shoulder.

"Carson?"

"Hello, brother."

The boy turned, and Jasper's heart lurched. It *was* Carson, but not as Jasper remembered him. In his memory, his brother had jade-colored eyes and hair like wildfire. This version of Carson, this *thing*, had a gray-toothed smile and irises stained pure black.

He offered his hand. "C'mon, Jasp, I want to show you something."

Jasp. The name rang like a bell in his mind. Only one person had ever called him that.

Only one.

They walked for a time, though Jasper knew not where, through clumps of dead forest and strands of bracken until they reached a small, still pond. Across the water, a tire swing hung from the branch of a gum tree, ticking mindlessly in the breeze.

A sense of dread overtook Jasper. He'd been here before.

"You remember this place, don't you, Jasp? I still come here on occasion, even though it makes me sad."

"Where are we?" Jasper asked.

Carson gave him a hint of a smile. "You know where we are." He waved at a slice of rock on the far bank. "That's where you and me played soldiers with your popgun. And that's"—he pointed at a stretch of sand shaped like a crescent moon—"where you killed me when I broke it."

The memory hit Jasper like a load of buckshot to the jaw.

The two of them chasing each other through the reeds, Carson clutching Jasper's popgun and waving it wildly above his head. Jasper yelling at him to slow down, to be careful with it because the gun was the last thing their father had given Jasper before drinking himself to death. Carson laughing and running faster. Jasper grinding his teeth as Carson fell, the gun snapping in half beneath his weight. Jasper on top of him, reaching for Carson's neck.

"Why'd you do that! Why?"

Carson choking, flailing at Jasper's wrists. Jasper squeezing harder...Carson's cheeks turning red, purple, blue.

"Jasp...s-stop. I can't—I can't...breathe."

The first person he'd ever killed, his brother.

Jasper's eyes filled with tears. "I'm sorry. I didn't mean to do it."

Carson stared across the pond. "But you did. And you lied about it. You told everyone I drowned."

"Shit, Carson, I was just a kid."

"So was I." His face darkened. "It's all I'll ever be."

A cold gust of wind swept across the water, and Jasper watched in horror as Carson dissolved, his head coming apart first, followed by his neck, torso, and waist, every part of him dissolving until Jasper was left holding a handful of ash.

A swelling sensation filled his skull and forced his gaze to the water. There, a reflection rippled. A man he didn't recognize stared back at him. Liver spots peppered his cheeks, and his forehead was wrinkled with lines deep enough to be razor cuts. From his head spilled fine tangles of greasy hair, and he had a mouth packed with rows of broken teeth. Streams of black fluid ran from his eyes and bled over the ruined landscape of his face.

"No," Jasper whispered.

"Yes," the man in the water replied.

Jasper spun and barreled through the brush, branches tearing at his arms and tangling his feet. One caught him across the eye and shredded the fragile meat of his cheek, but he kept running.

And running.

And running…

Through the pain and blood.

Across fields of reeking muck, the mud sucking at his boots, his ankles.

Running until he reached the base of a hollow birch where he collapsed with his fingers jammed deep into his ears and his eyes screwed shut. There, he screamed until his voice tore. He cried until sleep took him and filled his head with the faces of the people he'd killed. People who no longer looked like people, but rather creatures with rotten jaws who shrieked and pulled him apart in a sea of black-toothed smiles.

The man woke encased in vines.

A carpet of yellow jessamine wound over his legs, a mound of cat's claw around his chest. Creepers twined through his hair and filled his mouth, extending lower to coat the walls of his throat. A surge of bile set him to thrashing against the plants, ripping them away in handfuls as he struggled to his knees. His eyes felt bleary and unfocused, his arms and legs weak. He ran a hand over his face and fingered the cord of scar tissue there as he tried to remember. Anything.

A thought rose, a creed from another life.

Follow the moss north. Find help.

It seemed as good a plan as any.

So he did, but the moss lied to him and sent him in circles. At times, he smelled campfire smoke and heard voices trickle through the fog, only to find himself back where he'd started, staring at the empty black hollow carved in the base of the birch tree.

Still, he walked.

Hunger pangs set him to digging beetles from the bark of papyrus trees. Bouts of thirst followed—ones he quenched with rancid gulps of stagnant water that roiled his stomach. His thoughts bled into one another until all that mattered was the next step, the next aching breath. Soon, even that didn't matter much.

Yet, something carried him forward.

The memory of an old man. The one who'd led him here and banished him to this steaming hell, wherever *here* was.

After a length of time he could not discern, he stumbled upon a break in the trees. There shuffled a figure in a tattered duster, moving slowly toward a warm bloom of light on the horizon.

The thing once called Jasper followed and soon found himself standing upon a rough patch of cobblestone. It was a square, and a broad one at that, jammed with faces hidden behind porcelain masks. A group of women regarded him suspiciously from beneath a striped awning. They wore ruffled skirts replete with garter belts and stockings, and their lips were painted in bright, stinging reds.

Whores, he thought, though the word held little meaning for him.

He searched the crowd for the old man he'd seen through the trees and spotted him ascending a set of wooden steps across the square.

Through the bodies, he pushed. Up the steps, past a broad set of swinging doors, and into a wall of noise: laughter mixed with the bright clinking of beer mugs. An accordion sang from the corner. The place stank of brine and smoke. He paid the scent no mind.

He was searching…for someone.

Across the room ran a broad oak bar packed with the rough-looking sort, men who kept their heads buried in their drinks and their hands near their pistols. Among them, seated in the middle, he spotted a familiar pair of shoulders and a duster he recognized; only, it seemed newer, cleaner. A set of eyes reflected back at him from the mirror.

He knew those eyes.

They belonged to the man who'd shot…whom? He couldn't recall. And then, suddenly, he did.

Dylan. His nephew's name had been Dylan.

Jasper raised his gun…and fired.

THE CROWING

1386

I mark my age in scars. A forest of white lines mar my forearm, and tomorrow, the day of the Crowing, the hags will cut the final one. Tomorrow, I am to die having never once glimpsed the color of the sky.

A foot in the ribs wakes me, followed by a harsh cackle. My eyes creak open to Mother Valérie gripping a torch, the light dripping across the floor of my cave-made-prison in dusty orange puddles. A cruel smile parts her beautiful lips.

"On your feet, Ronyan! The Black Well awaits."

Ronyan. The Old Crows' name for me, an insult given the scabs that fester my skin and pock my face. The welts and sores that ooze and blister no matter how I tend to them. Though I am only eighteen, I have a spine as crooked as a spinster's, with hair white as frost and skin wrinkled like a leather pouch. The Crowing requires the blood of a royal, and after thirteen years held captive, mine is nearly spent.

I grunt and look away.

"Ahh, feeling feisty, are we, girl? I've no time for your obstinance this morn."

I steel myself for another kick, but instead, she jams the torch into the flank of the goat lying next to me. Hob's screams mix with mine as I push to my knees and grasp her robes. "Please, Mother Valérie, do not harm him. I will do as you say."

Her eyes narrow, and she clucks her tongue. She is centuries old and beautiful beyond measure, her youth stolen bit by bit from mine and the royals the Crows bled before me. "That you will, Ronyan. That you will." She pulls a length of rope from her pocket and flings it at me. "Bind this filthy creature and come. It is time." With a flourish, she turns and stomps outside, a purple cloak trimmed in silver trailing behind her.

I crouch next to Hob and examine the wound. It has already blistered, the hair charred into a pocked ring. I stroke his coat, and he stops licking the burn long enough to give me a soft bleat. I trace my fingers the length of his jaw and then cup his face. His rectangular pupils quiver in place.

"I'm sorry, Hob. Their hate should not fall upon you."

But it will. They will bleed him first.

With a heavy heart, I loop the rope around his neck and give it a tug. He follows without hesitation, even now, marching to his death.

I have never had a finer friend.

I step from the cave and into the swirling fog that has swallowed Francia's sky for a millennium. It is the curse of the Old Crows, a veil so they may hunt unseen, frail shadows painted on the bedchamber walls of Carcassonne's children—there one moment and gone with the child the next.

They took me from the palace when I was five. Thirteen years later, the memory is like a fever dream: Father in our chamber, facing Mother Madeleine with his broadsword drawn, the emerald hilt flashing in the moonlight, Mother Madeleine staring back with her flawless hands wrapped tight around my neck and that of my brother Thomason's, neither of us able to move…to breathe. I can still hear her voice drifting like ice down my spine.

The sky is dark, and the hills are white, both in death as in life. Bring to me a royal's line, for in it, I shall make your kingdom mine. Where there are two, there must be one. Give us thy daughter or give us thy son.

And Father cast his cold, pale eyes on me.

Take the girl if you must.

I bury his hateful voice and hobble after Mother Valérie, every step sending bolts of pain through my ruined feet. The fog lessens as we near the witches' camp: a sea of shining tents and the apothecary full of glass jars packed with various herbs and roots. I know some of their names and uses. Acacia to steal a baby from its mother's womb. Hellebore or maleficium to fly. Nightshade to poison.

Beyond the apothecary, at the edge of the encampment, lie the dead woods—a dense maze of fog-scrubbed bark and desiccated branches. When the Old Crows first brought me here to Salt Rock, Mother Grimilda spoke of the Otherlings, the ageless creatures the Crows seduced and banished within. It was Otherling blood that forged the Black Well, she said, and it is only Otherling blood that can reclaim it.

Sometimes, in the early morning hours, I can hear them shriek. Distant, haunting cries muffled by the fog that crawl across my skin like a nest of spiders. There's a hunger to them, a seething, bubbling rage that bathes the witches in fear. They tell me I am never to speak of the Otherlings, never to mention their name or it will cost me my tongue.

It is said only a Crow may enter the dead woods and survive, and that anyone daft enough to do so will be devoured alive. But I know something different, because I've been in the forest, and I've seen an Otherling with my own eyes. A creature with skin black as the night sky and teeth like metal who spared my life in exchange for a promise—one I intend to fulfill today.

We break from the tents, and I hear the grating whispers of the Old Crows dripping through the air. They gather on either side of the first bone arch, the witches lining the cobblestone path in their ritual garb. Black cloaks clasped at the neck with silver brooches, banks of raven hair pinned in place with bone taken from sparrows. I am ugly in comparison, the old crone from a child's storybook, and if one were to see me now, they would think me the witch.

The Crows fall silent as I hobble forward and brace myself for what comes next. A hot glob of spit smacks my cheek. A warm cup of urine soaks my tunic. My eyes water against the bitter ammonia stench. A handful of rocks flung with force bite into my neck and shoulders. A stone cracks off my shin and sends a sheet of blood running down my calf.

They hurl insults with perfectly shaped lips.

"Bent-nose swine!"

"Wanton whore!"

"Vile filth!"

Fingers tear at my hair as more spit spatters my face. Hob bleats in terror behind me, yanking against the rope with flared nostrils. I go numb inside and force myself to continue. My joints ache as if they are stuffed with glass. At last, I reach the final bone arch with its forest of cracked antlers and press beneath it into the great amphitheater. At its center, bound to the iron latticework encircling Salt Rock, are the children.

There are always four—one for each of the seasons. This year there are three girls and a boy, all of them younger than ten, some closer to five. They stand gagged, their bodies cloaked in simple linen gowns. I do not know the girls, peasants by the looks of them, with ash-smudged cheeks and hair caked in dirt, but the boy's face is unblemished, something familiar about his square jaw and high cheekbones, his tuft of auburn hair. Before I can place it, Mother Valérie jams her gnarled cane into my back.

"Onward, Ronyan. No time to dally."

With quaking legs, I limp over the elaborate wings scorched into the amphitheater floor, the fan-shaped tail and curved beak, and ascend the white stone steps to Salt Rock. The Black Well rises from the stone's center. I can smell it, a stale copper scent that churns in my stomach. Hob smells it, too, bleating and jerking against the rope. I kneel and coax him next to me as the Crows filter in one by one. Their voices crackle with excitement as they take their places, their strength withered after a year without innocent blood.

Mother Madeleine steps forward wearing her feathered headdress and raises her hands.

"Be still, my sisters, be still!"

The buzzing stops.

"Today, on this most sacred of all days, we remember the torment and suffering of those who came before us; the brave sisters who were hanged or burned or torn asunder by the evil men of the south for nothing more than practicing their beliefs. *Our* beliefs."

Murmurs ripple through the coven. Heads nod.

"Today, as we have for a thousand years, we offer the children of Carcassonne to the Black Well as vengeance. With its power, we will renew the fog that chokes their kingdom and holds our enemies at bay. We will drape them in everlasting darkness and"—she levels a long finger at me, then draws it toward the boy—"drink the last drops of youth from their royal daughter and start anew with their princeling son."

A hundred lungs expel as one, the sound like an ocean tide scrubbing sand.

"My Black Sisters, remove thy cloaks!"

Shrouds fall to reveal a sea of milk-white skin. Legs and waists and breasts coated in gooseflesh.

Mother Madeleine slips a sickle from her sleeve and disrobes, the blade shining as she raises her arms overhead once more. "Let the Crowing begin!"

A low reverberating *bom*... *bom*... *bom* fills the amphitheater, the Crows at the base of each of the five marble pillars swinging thick elk-bone drumsticks. The sound vibrates my teeth as Mother Madeleine drags one of the girls forward by the hair. She squeals and Mother Madeleine snaps her head back to reveal a soft patch of throat.

"Shh, you stupid thing. Calm now, and I may yet spare thee."

It is a lie, but the girl goes still all the same, urine soaking her gown, fear clouding her gaze. Mother Madeleine nods toward the Crows standing naked before her and begins the chant.

"So what is above, we send below, for the life that is hers, we shall reap with a crow."

The coven echoes the verse, their voices shrill and ragged.

"So what is above, we send below, for the life that is hers, we shall reap with a crow."

And they crow.

"Ah...Ah...Ahhh."

It is the sound that has infested my nightmares for more than a decade. It starts slow, and then builds to a biting, inhuman cadence; a wall of shrieking noise that spills through my veins. The girl's eyes flash to mine a moment before Mother Madeleine carves a red grin into her neck and thrusts her into the well.

She repeats the ritual, wrestling the second girl forward. This one thrashes and screams, stopping only when the sickle parts her esophagus. The last girl flaps her hands and faints a second before Mother Madeleine slits her throat. My eyes burn as she topples into the well. Mother Madeleine smears the girl's blood across her breasts and flashes me a gleaming smile.

"Bring me the beast."

My stomach tears. I do not want Hob to die. He is my family and my only friend. But I have no choice, for it is with his death I hope to win my freedom. With a sinking dread, I limp forward and offer her the rope.

"Ahh, Ronyan, you sod. Today we begin with you."

She snatches my wrist and jerks me to her chest, the sickle coming to rest against my neck. My heart explodes. This is not the way, *cannot* be the way. Hob must die first. In all my years, I have never bled before the animal. My gaze falls upon the Black Well. A billow of acrid heat drifts upward, wet with rot, and my legs go weak. A memory flashes. The Otherling I met in the dead forest. The thing that found me at the base of a withered cypress when I escaped Salt Rock a year ago, its finger tracing across my cheek as it spoke.

Allow me to bind my blood with that of the beast's, then return to the Crows for their feast. Pour my blood into the well and light the fire that will summon hell. Until that time remain unseen, and when you call, we shall make you our queen.

It felt like a dream, the thing slowly drawing a talon across its wrist before setting it to Hob's mouth, Hob lapping at the Otherling's blood until his tongue blackened. I fainted then and woke to Mother Grimilda staring down with her spiteful gaze. She dragged me back by my hair and threatened to carve out my eyes. I begged her not to, swore an oath to never again flee. She smiled and said she wouldn't. She cut off my toes instead.

"Sisters," Mother Madeleine cries, her breath hot in my ear, "let us drink what youth yet remains in this pitiful creature."

I go rigid as the knife digs into my throat.

It cannot happen. It must not.

She begins the chant. "So what is above, we send below, for the life that is hers, we shall reap with a—"

A sudden rush of air skims my cheek, and the sickle falls from my neck. I whirl around to see Mother Madeleine crumple with an arrow protruding from her eye, the shaft fletched with green and gold.

The colors of the king...

A horn blows a haunting, solitary tone. More join it, followed by a great roar and the thunder of hooves. Rows of armor flash dull at the edges of the amphitheater.

"Ready," a voice cries. "Release!"

A storm of arrows rain from the sky and plunge into naked flesh. An Old Crow, one I recognize as Mother Renée, is hacked down near the sacrificial stone, blood streaming over her forehead and into her hateful eyes. Another Crow, one with raven feathers wound through her flaxen hair, bares her teeth and charges a soldier wielding a broadsword, only to be cleaved from behind by a battle-axe. A sea of blades spills through the Crows, men hacking and slashing, killing those who fight back and binding those who don't.

A man in a silver crown ascends the steps of Salt Rock. He is broad-shouldered, with piercing blue eyes, and dressed in a cloak bearing the royal crest of my family—a golden lion spitting a tongue of fire upon a grass-green field. My pulse races. I cannot believe what I am seeing, *who* I am seeing, for before me stands my brother, Thomason.

He strides for the boy and cuts him loose. The child wobbles into his arms with a cry, wrapping his still pudgy arms around Thomason's neck.

"Ah, Faustin, my boy," Thomason says. "Fret not, for we were never far. Sir Jean lay in wait for a fortnight to track the vile Crow who stole you. And here you are found and returned to me safe."

With a gasp, I rush forward and grasp my brother's cloak.

"Thomason, is it truly thee?"

My answer comes as a gauntlet to the temple.

"Do not presume to touch me, crone."

I scatter back, and his eyes scan the deep lines etched into my face and the pockets of sagging flesh planted beneath my eyes.

"What evil is this?" he says. "How is it you know me?"

"Thomason, it is I, your sister Cateline."

He strikes me again, harder, and I taste blood. "Do *not* let that name pass your lips again, witch, or I will carve out your tongue." He crouches in front of me, his eyes simmering with contempt. "Now, I will ask you again. How is it you know me?"

"Because Father had hair as red as yours and Mother colored your eyes."

"Lies." His beard twitches and he glances toward a nearby spearman. "Bind her. We will burn her in Carcassonne with the rest."

"Yes, milord."

The man jerks me to my feet.

"Wait, sire," I cry. "I can end it. I can end the curse. I can bring back the sun."

Thomason pauses, and I expect him to continue down the steps, but he returns and places a steel-tipped finger beneath my chin and tilts my gaze to his. "And why pray tell, should I believe the lies of a Crow?"

"Because I am no Crow, my lord. I too was once like your boy, a child with dreams of seeing the sky before the hags stole me away. I wish nothing more than to see their curse burn."

His eyes turn to slits, and he cocks his head. "I will grant you your wish, but whatever you are, creature, know this. I will not be mocked. If you indeed lie, I shall see to it you are flayed and strung upon the racks." He nods at the spearman with a smirk. "Release her. We shall have our amusement."

The man loosens his grip, and I scurry toward the corpse of Mother Madeleine. I pry the blood-stained sickle from her rigid fingers and then approach Hob and ease my arms beneath his soft belly. It takes all of my remaining strength to lift and set him upon the well's rim. He gives me a sorrowful look, his legs trembling, and my vision blurs. I do not want to do what comes next.

I press my forehead to his and take in a slow, jagged breath.

"Be brave, my dear friend," I whisper. "Be brave."

And I cut his throat.

He squeals. Blood spurts from his neck in a fine red mist that quickly darkens to something like tar, a black, viscous substance that stains my shift and drenches the stone. With a sob, I gently roll him into the well.

"What farce is this?" Thomason says, spreading his arms. "Do you take me for a fool, wench? The mere blood of a goat to appease a thousand-year curse?"

I stand to face him and think once more of the Otherling's whispered words, of its finger drifting across my cheek, cold as a winter spring.

"No, sire. I do not."

He waves to the spearman. "Seize the cursed bitch."

The man takes no more than a step before the first rumble hits. A sudden shearing rises beneath my feet. Cracks splinter outward from the well and race across the amphitheater. Soldiers and Crows slam to the ground. Great slivers of rock break from the stone spires and crush those unlucky enough to be caught beneath. Shrieks of pain split the air. Cries rise all around me. The cracks widen and spear outward through the amphitheater walls, carving jagged black gorges in their wake. It continues for what feels like an eternity, the earth grinding in place, the amphitheater walls crumbling into great plumes of dust and rock.

And then silence.

A blanket of pulverized limestone scorches my nostrils and coats my tongue.

The earth creaks and groans.

Without warning, a tremor greater than the rest shears through Salt Rock. A column of brilliant green light explodes from the Black Well and blooms outward across the sky in a radiant halo.

I have no time to marvel. A crackling bolt of green fire peels from the pillar and strikes my chest. Agony rips through my body. More bolts of green flame branch across the amphitheater to impale the Crows, both living and dead alike. I lock eyes with Mother Valérie, who watches me in horror as her face smokes and peels. Mother Grimilda's mouth unbuckles in a silent scream, her tongue rippling with green veins of light before dissolving entirely. And not just her. *All* of them—every Crow paralyzed and crumbling into ash.

The pain in my chest transforms to a sudden warmth. I watch in wonder as the boils peppering my arms firm to smooth flesh. A prickling sensation spreads across my feet, toes sprouting from the nubs Mother Grimilda's paring knife left behind. My spine pops and straightens until I can once again stand tall. My vision sharpens. The scent of smoke, sulfur, and ash invades my nostrils. My fingertips prod cheeks that have grown soft and full. I pull a length of hair from my shoulders and gasp at the color, the delicate red of my youth.

I cannot move, cannot speak, for I have been remade.

With a sudden *whoosh*, the column of flame flickers and snaps out.

Weapons clatter to the stone all around me. Shields and bows. I look for Thomason in a daze and find him on his knees next to his son, tears streaming into his beard as he gazes skyward in awe. They are all like that, every soldier staring up at a sight not seen for centuries: a lemon-yellow sun piercing a crisp blue sky. It is why they do not spot the black things creeping from the dead forest.

They are creatures twice as tall as any man with hands splintered into eight talon-tipped fingers. They move in crouched silence, tendons leaping across rivers of muscle, their teeth bared in jagged lines.

A soldier shouts and takes his feet with a call to arms. Horns blare. Sharp metal is drawn. It is too late. The Otherlings sweep through the soldiers with frightening speed, disemboweling the men, severing limbs and heads in between shrieks of terror and cries of pain. Thomason's men flee and scatter, and he watches in a daze as they are slaughtered one by one. Soon, he and his son are all that remain.

"Thomason," I say, approaching him.

He looks at me, blinking hard.

"C-Cateline?"

"Yes, Thomason, it is I." My voice is light and without strain. I barely recognize it as my own.

He attempts to stand but is forced back down by the Otherling who found me in the dead forest. His talons click off Thomason's chain mail, his voice leaking out like a wisp of smoke.

"What is to become of this thing, my Queen?"

Thomason's eyes flash, and I see in them Father's hatred: Father as he beat me in my bedchamber while Thomason watched…and laughed. Father who looked upon me with derision and scorn, a girl instead of an heir. Father who all too gladly fed me to the Crows in Thomason's place and whose cruelty drove Mother to take her own life.

With a steady hand, I set a finger beneath his chin as he did mine, mockingly, and tilt it higher. "You have grown cruel as Father, Thomason. You would have had me burned."

His eyes widen. "No! I knew not it was you, dear sister. The knight's guard scoured the land for months in search of you. We all thought you dead."

His mouth twitches, and I know it is a lie.

"Please, I beg of thee, spare my life, and that of my son, your nephew. We shall leave at once."

The boy looks up at me through a sheen of tears, and I nearly break. He is innocent as I once was, but I know with time the boy prince would come to hate me as his father does, and his father before him. I kneel and pull him to me, then take the jeweled sword at Thomason's waist and slide it from the scabbard.

"I will grant you your request, brother. You and your son shall live, but you will wish you hadn't. You will not leave this place. You shall exist as I have, in the dark alone. And you shall watch your son learn to love me in your place."

I nod at the Otherlings restraining him. "Take him away."

Thomason's face lines with rage, and he roars as they drag him from the amphitheater. His son cries and squirms beneath my arm, but I hold him close until he calms.

The Otherling from the dead forest eases next to me, its voice sliding out in a hiss. "What next, my Queen?"

My gaze drops to Thomason's sword, the emerald hilt sparkling in my hand, and I think of the great walled city of my youth. *Carcassonne.* I stare back out over the now unblemished horizon, past the death and slaughter of the amphitheater, and I know my answer.

"We will take back what is mine."

SHADOW PUPPETS

I'm not sure what wakes me. Maybe it's the low thrum of the diesel engine vibrating the walls, or the cold cone of light spilling across my trailer park ceiling at two in the morning. Whatever it is, it pulls me toward the window, groggy-eyed and yawning.

I part the blinds, expecting to see some grumbling semi-driver clunking another mobile home into place, but instead, I see *her*. She climbs from an old Ford F-150—toeing the ground like it's a thin sheet of ice, first one foot and then the other—easing from the seat with a quick glance up at the streetlight. I think she's around my age, fifteen, or maybe a bit younger. Her eyes are encased in a heart-shaped face, her features delicate with an upturned nose centered over a chin that looks carved from glass. Something about her reminds me of the porcelain dolls Mom keeps stashed on the top shelf of her closet, the ones trimmed in lace with their skin glazed and shining.

A heavy *thunk!* pulls my gaze to the driver's side door. A man stands there, huge, with a pair of meat-slab arms and a bald head glittering with sweat. He stares at the girl for a long moment, then spits and pulls a blanket from the bed of the truck, spreading it carefully over the girl's head like he thinks the streetlight will give her a sunburn. A slow rising heat fills my chest as he shoves her roughly toward the mobile home.

I know his type: the kind of guy who posts up on the porch with a forty and a fat wad of chew stuffed in his lower lip, ready to have a go at his kids or his wife just for looking at him wrong. *Light his fuse and watch him explode.* Dad was that kind of guy before he abandoned me and Mom to the trailer park. It never took much.

I watch them disappear into the trailer with my breath fogging the glass. Something about the girl bothers me. The slack expression and the downcast eyes, the way she wrapped her arms around her chest like maybe even breathing was too much work. It made me want to rush outside and give her a hug, to tell her everything would be okay. *And that's what it is,* I decide, identifying the thing bothering me: *I've never seen someone so sad before.*

I'm up early the next morning and catch her dad, or whoever he is, hanging blackout curtains in the trailer's windows. A thick beard crawls up his neck, one I imagine to be teeming with cockroaches and beetles and various other sorts of shelled insects. His eyes are crooked, buried too close to the bridge of his nose, and his cheeks are lumpy, like maybe whatever god put him together had a few too many drinks beforehand. His gaze twitches up and down as he works—glazed, one eyelid stretched wider than the other.

After a bit, I close the blinds and wander into the kitchen for breakfast. Mom is humming and swaying in front of a frying pan, eggs sizzling, wearing the threadbare purple robe Dad gave her two Christmases ago.

I sit down and trace my finger over an ancient syrup stain on the checkered tablecloth. "We have new neighbors."

"Oh, yeah? Who's that?"

"Some girl and her dad."

She spins around. "A girl, huh? Your age?"

"I think so."

She arches an eyebrow and gives me a half-smile.

"What?" I ask, feigning confusion. Valley Acres isn't exactly teeming with teenagers, especially girls. Mostly, we've got a bunch of elementary kids playing in the dirt until their parents can afford a better school district.

"Well, then," she says, "we better make them some cookies, don't you think?"

I carry the tin over around noon, waving at our nosy neighbor, Mrs. Amblin, as I cross the street. She waves back from her lawn chair, a vodka tonic already sprouting from her sun-damaged hand. She treats the trailer park like it's a soap opera (which, to be fair, it mostly is), hoping to catch a neighborhood argument or two, or an affair if she's lucky. Anything she can use to pass the time and fill her gossip jar.

Her gaze crawls over the back of my neck as I amble up the steps of the girl's trailer, hesitating for a moment when I spot the light fixture. It's been blacked out, glazed in a thick coat of paint. A few hasty splotches splattered and dripped down the door frame. I stare at the mess, confused, then knock once, twice, three times before the bolt clicks and the door inches open.

"What'cha want?" a voice asks with all the warmth of a growl.

"Hi, I, uh…my name's Kyle. I brought you guys these." I raise the cookies. "Welcome to the neighborhood."

My smile comes out as a quick twitch of my lips before the door widens and the man steps out. He's even bigger up close, his gut leaking over a pair of worn jean shorts, a greasy handprint smeared across the thigh. He says nothing, only stares down at me with his mud-colored eyes and his arms crossed. I think he's going to tell me to screw off, but instead, he reaches out with a meaty palm to snatch the tin.

"You live around here, kid?"

"Just across the street," I say, my gaze drifting behind him into the dim interior of the trailer. I see her there, the girl, buried in a pool of shadow. Her hand flutters up in a wave, and I raise my hand to return the gesture, but the man steps back inside with a half-mumbled *thanks,* and slams the door shut before I can.

"Hah!" Mrs. Amblin calls from across the street. "Guess they won't be coming to any neighborhood barbeques!"

I roll my eyes at her, annoyed…but hopeful too, because I'm pretty sure the girl smiled at me before the door closed.

A few nights later, I sneak back across the street with a handful of pebbles and toss one at her window. I'm coiled behind the hedgerow, ready to run if her dad appears, but on my fourth try, the curtains part, and I exhale as she peeks through. I stand and raise a hand, feeling stupid, like I'm in one of Mom's cheesy romantic comedies, the idiot kid waving up at the girl from the lawn—except in this version I'm only a few feet away, and I'm pretty sure if he saw me, the girl's dad would kill me.

She cracks her window, her face framed by an oil slick of dark hair. "What are you doing?"

"I, um, never got your name. From the other day."

Her eyes narrow. "I never gave it."

"Yeah. Sorry…it's just—"

"Winter."

"Huh?"

"My name is Winter."

Beautiful. *Winter.* It fits. "I'm Kyle."

"I know. I heard."

"Oh…right." *Idiot.*

The corners of her lips curl higher, and I can't help but notice that her skin's the color of moonlight.

"So," I say, trying to recover, "me and some friends are heading up to the lake in the morning. You wanna tag along and meet a few of the other kids around here?"

Her smile wilts. "I…can't."

"Why not?"

"My dad…he won't—"

A pair of headlights flash over my shoulder and send her scurrying into the dark of her room. She reappears a moment after they pass, her face tight and her gaze ticking over the road behind me. "I just can't. I gotta go. My dad might hear us. Thanks for the cookies, though."

"Wait. You maybe want to talk again sometime? Like this?"

Her forehead tightens, and she pulls a slice of cheek between her teeth with a tentative nod. "Sure, I'd like that. Tomorrow. But wait until eleven, okay? My dad is usually passed out by then."

With that, she disappears, and I float back to my trailer helium-happy, struggling to focus on anything other than my rapidly beating heart.

The day passes like quicksand. I skip the lake and help Mom patch a hole in the drywall that's the size of Dad's fist, another memory of him sanded away. *Good riddance.* If only it were always so easy—a bit of sandpaper and some elbow grease, so she could forget him forever. But I know she can't. His shadow is buried in the curve of her once-broken nose and the way she flinches at sudden sounds like he might leap out of the closet at any minute, fists bared.

Bastard.

I hope he stays gone forever. If he doesn't, I don't know what I'll do. I don't like to think about it. All I know is I'll never let him hurt Mom again.

After dinner, I kill a few hours playing Xbox and then tick off the rest by watching the hour hand circle the clock in my room. When it hits eleven, I slip through the living room past Mom, who's snoring away in front of some late-night talk show, and make my way outside and across the street. Winter is waiting for me this time, her window sliding open at my approach.

"Hey," she says.

"Hi," I reply, my palms already sweating. "So, we—" I nod toward her dad's room. "Are we, uh, good?"

She tucks a glossy lock of hair behind her ear. "Yeah. He's asleep."

A warm buzz runs through me. *We have time...*

"So, where you from?" I ask.

The answer is Stockbridge, Massachusetts, and this is her fifth move in the last four years. She likes indie music and fried pickles, and wants to travel to Alaska someday to see the glaciers and the humpbacks.

I tell her a little about myself. How I can't wait to graduate and move to Austin to start a career in computer programming—do anything other than work in the oil fields like Dad did before he left.

The next night, I talk about him a little, too. Tell her how he chased some greasy-haired waitress to Houston and how me and Mom are better off with him gone. She goes quiet for a bit, listening to me, then fills me in on how her mom died of cancer when she was five and how she inherited her mother's allergy to the sun. It has something to do with ultraviolet light; it's the reason her dad won't let her out of the trailer, because she'll burn in seconds. She says he cares, that he always does what's best for her, but the way her mouth tightens when she talks about him gives me doubts.

On the fourth night, she waves me closer with a playful flip of her wrist. "Hey, you wanna see something cool?"

I nod and edge through the shrubs next to her window. I feel my skin tingle being this close to her.

She fades into her room and swirls back after flipping on a small lamp near her bed. Scarlet light bleeds through the lampshade, painting the walls in a mix of crimson-pink tones. Her room is bare, save a few posters tacked here and there, one of a mare tossing its mane and another of Yosemite's Half Dome at sunrise.

"Watch this," she says, raising her hands. She laces her fingers together, and a shadow spreads over her door. It's a bird, something a kindergartner would draw in art class. But then she flutters her fingers and the shadow grows, transforming into a lush set of wings followed by a bloom of tailfeathers and a beak.

She curves her arms, hands flapping, and the shadow flies—*actually flies*—across her ceiling, the motion so fluid, so *lifelike*, I almost expect it to burst through her window.

Then, without warning, the shadow rips down over her wall straight toward me.

I stumble back and trip over a row of flowerpots at my feet. Several crash to the rocks. Winter flashes me an *Oh, God* look, her eyes snapping wide as a door smacks open down the hall.

"Go!" she hisses, whipping the curtains shut. I dive into the hedges instead. I don't have time to run since her old man would hear me for sure. He barrels into her room, his voice angry and dripping sleep.

"The hell's going on in here? Why's the window open?"

Winter says nothing, and I imagine her dad's concrete gaze surveying the walls, the floor, looking for something off, something not quite right. I hear her curtains tear open a second later, and I try to still my breathing despite the swarm of mosquitoes ravaging my neck. I twitch as one bites, and I'm sure he's seen me, is about to jump over the windowsill and snap my neck, when Winter speaks.

"I was hot. I needed some air."

Silence. Then: "And the pots?"

"I heard a cat. It—"

She's cut off by the unmistakable sound of a slap, flesh on flesh, followed by a sharp cry.

I cringe and ball my fists in my lap. Hard. *Asshole.*

"You're lying," he says, fury creeping into his voice. "Don't you lie to me."

"No, no. I promise. It was—"

"It's that boy, ain't it? The one that came by the other day. Don't think I didn't catch the way you were lookin' at him."

"N-no, Dad. I-I swear I wasn't—

"Bullshit."

The window slams down, and all I can do is sit there trembling with rage, thinking, *I will kill you if you touch her again. I will kill you, I will kill you, I will kill you.*

He boards up her window in the morning.

The sharp tack of nails in plywood wakes me, and I slump over to the blinds with my scalp prickling, wondering what the hell's going on. He's out there banging away as if what he's doing is as normal as picking weeds. I widen the blinds to get a better view, and the hammer stops mid-stroke, hanging there.

When he turns, his eyes are flat and black, like those of a trout. A nail juts from the corner of his mouth. He stares at me, unflinching, until a wave of nausea twists through my gut.

I glance down, unable to hold his gaze. When I look back again, he's gone.

"She's in trouble," I tell Mom at breakfast.

"Who?"

"The girl. Winter. Her dad's not right."

She pushes back from the table and reaches for the crumpled pack of Camel Lights on the counter, shakes one loose, and plants it between her lips. Lights it. "Hmm. How so?"

"He boarded over her window. We need to do something."

She takes a deep drag, the tip burning cherry-red. "Now, Kyle, you know we can't do that."

"Why not?"

"Cause it's none of our business, is it?" She grabs her plate and stands, apparently done with the conversation. "Now, help me clean up."

And there it is—the broken piece of her, the piece that kept Dad around long after she should have cut him loose.

I grab my plate and toss it in the sink, my fork clattering to the floor. She spins on me, voice sharp. "Kyle, what's gotten into…"

But I'm already gone, storming back to my room.

It doesn't take long to figure out his pattern.

Out of the trailer at seven-thirty, dressed in his faded-orange construction gear, tool belt strapped tight beneath his gut. Home by five.

I watch him for a couple days to make sure—gone at seven-thirty, home by five—before I decide to go over. The guy is punctual if nothing else.

Outside, the sky is cloudy, the air so thick with moisture that it feels like I'm walking through a bowl of chowder soup. Mrs. Amblin is already stretched out on her lawn chair, wearing a massive floppy sunhat and reading an old People magazine with a set of oversized sunglasses perched on the bridge of her nose. She pulls them down as I pass, flashing me her red lipstick smile, the one that says: *I'm watching...always watching.*

I wave at her—*nothing to see here*—and bound up Winter's steps.

She answers on the fourth knock, the door cracking open with a stale whiff of air. "Hey," she says, toeing a fringe of the orange shag spilling over the threshold.

"Hi, you maybe want to—"

The words die on my tongue when I spot the swamp of purple devouring her eye.

"He did that?"

She nods.

"Winter..."

Her eyes harden. "He was right to. There are things about me…us…you don't know."

"I know a father shouldn't hit his daughter." I say it with more force than I intend, the anger in my voice setting her back a step.

She eyes me like she sees something new, like maybe I'd hit her, too, if she made me mad enough.

"Look...I gotta go, Kyle," she says, moving to close the door. "I'm sorry I scared you."

"Wait," I say, planting a hand against the wood, "are you talking about the bird? Because that was the coolest thing I've ever seen." I'm not lying. It's all I've thought about the last few days, how the hell she did that—the rush of feathers and that liquid-smooth motion as it flew across the wall.

Her face lights up like a pale sunrise—that first warm glow of the day. I take a chance and grab her hand, her palm cool against mine as I tug her outside.

"What are you doing?" she asks, not really resisting.

"Let's go to the park for a bit. It's right down the street."

She looks skyward with a hard swallow. "I can't. The sun, it—"

"Won't do anything." I swing up the umbrella I brought, Mom's white and yellow-striped one. "And besides, it's cloudy today. No sun, see?" I step aside for her to look out, which she does with a quick glance up at the bank of clouds foaming overhead.

"I don't know..."

"C'mon," I plead, "when's the last time you had some fun?"

"It's been...a while."

I give her my best puppy-dog eyes and curl my hands over my chest like a set of paws. "P-p-please."

She giggles and blows at her bangs with a sigh. "Yeah, okay. But only for a few minutes."

The park is busier than I've seen in ages, the playground buzzing with kids. Moms fringe the sides and chat in clusters of twos and threes. Dogs wheel over the grass, chasing after orange and yellow frisbees. A group of knobby-kneed sixth-graders smash into each other, playing flag football.

I lead Winter away from all the chaos. We sit on a bench nestled next to a huge birch tree. It takes a good five minutes for her shoulders to unclench, and five more before she stops glancing up at the sky like she half-expects to catch fire.

Then she's staring at me with those dazzling blue eyes of hers, little flecks of green swimming through her irises like glitter.

"Thanks," she says. "I needed this." Her hand slips into mine, and my heart beats a little faster.

"I figured."

We stay like that, hand in hand, quiet, listening to the leaves rustle with the breeze, while I work up the courage to ask her the question that's been bothering me since she moved in. When I finally do, my voice nearly cracks.

"Are you...okay? I mean, with your dad and all?"

She blinks, sighs. "He means well. He's a little overprotective after what happened to Mom."

"With the cancer?"

Her eyebrows arch like she doesn't know what I'm talking about, then settle quickly back into place. "Cancer? Yeah, I mean, sort of, but it's more than that. It's..." She rubs her arms and glances around like she's just realized she's outside. "I-I can't talk about it. I...should go. I'm sorry, Kyle, this was a mistake. I'm not safe for you."

My mouth unhinges as she stands. *Not safe for you?* I'm about to apologize and tell her I overstepped when a football thumps down near the bench. A boy runs up to retrieve it, his cheeks puffing red beneath a pile of rice-colored hair.

"Sorry," he says, bending to grab it. "We were just..." His eyes flick first at Winter and then at me, his mouth agape.

"Wh-what is that?" he asks, pointing at Winter's feet.

It takes me a moment to see what he does. Winter's shadow is rippling in the grass, moving like the surface of a pond disturbed by a rock. I blink at it and rub my eyes.

It's still there when I open them, but wavering, expanding across the turf like an anorexic version of Winter. The arms are unnaturally long, the fingertips wire-thin and quivering.

She gasps and stumbles sideways, tripping as she does. The umbrella flies from her hand and her shadow writhes in the sudden spray of light, boiling as tongues of flame spark around its edges. She scrambles back, back, back, pulling the shadow with her, the shadow growing in size, an arm slithering through the grass toward the boy.

It's then I realize that the sun has burned through the clouds.

A flurry of thin-as-bone fingers curl over the boy's shin and slide up his thigh. His mouth peels open in a shriek a second before he rips past me through the grass toward the shadow's jaw.

"Help me! *Help me!*"

I dive for his hand and seize a handful of his shirt instead.

He jerks to a stop, and I struggle to hold on as my forearm rivers with veins. The boy's eyes bulge, the stitches of his sleeve tearing one by one, *snick, snick, snick,* and then he's gone, catapulting across the turf toward the thing's mouth. His feet dissolve first, followed by his legs and waist. I lie in the grass stupefied, watching what's left of him sinking lower, turning to a fine carbon mist.

"Run, Kyle! *Run!*"

Winter's voice cuts through the fog in my brain like an electric current.

I jerk upright and lurch away from the shadow, slamming back down again as a searing heat bleeds through my ankle.

I roll over to see Winter scrambling for the umbrella, but she can't gain any traction, the shadow somehow anchoring her in place.

My hands tear out chunks of grass as the shadow drags me closer, slivers of dirt carving out beneath my fingernails. Panic surges up my throat as my foot nears its maw.

And plunges in.

The pain is incredible, like my leg is being dunked into a pot of boiling water so hot it feels cold.

Sparks flicker through my vision, and I almost pass out.

A blur of motion cuts in front of me toward Winter, a figure with tree-trunk arms carrying a blanket. His eyes are close-set, his bald head shining in the sun.

The pressure in my calf releases, and I look down to...nothing. No foot, no shin, just a pile of charred, oozing flesh and bits of ash drifting higher, spinning toward a quickly blurring sky.

The police question me in the hospital a week after I wake up. They grill me until a nurse orders them out with a snide, "That's enough. He's in no shape for this."

It isn't until I'm discharged that they drag me downtown for a second round: *No, officer, I don't know what happened to the girl or her father. No, sorry, I have no clue about their last name—I wish I did. Yes, the boy dissolved into a shadow, same as my leg...*

In the end, I guess they have too many corresponding witness accounts, too many strange descriptions of what happened, to charge me with the boy's disappearance, or charge anyone else for that matter. All they have are a bunch of nonsensical statements and a grief-stricken mother in search of answers that will never come.

I know because I want them myself.

The letter arrives six months later. I'm out on the porch sipping a tall glass of lemonade when the mailman spots me. He glances at my stub knee, then the envelope in his hand, and brings it up the steps. "I think this is for you," he says, handing it to me with a look I've grown accustomed to: a blend of pity and relief. Pity for me. Relief it isn't him.

I hold the letter in my hands as he shambles away. The envelope's wrinkled, the top of the address—*Kyle Carrington, 11080 Swallow Way*—smudged in spots, like whoever wrote it down was crying. I carefully slit the crease and pull out the piece of paper folded inside.

Kyle,

It's hard for me to write this. After what I did to you and that boy, there are no words. Nothing I can say or do will fix things.

All I know is you made me happy, and all I did was hurt you.

It's all I've ever done, really, just hurt people. Especially the ones I love. My mom. My dad. You...

He saved you, you know, my dad did. He brought you to the hospital after that old woman across the street told him where we'd gone.

I read the rest of it—my eyes pouring over every word, every letter, my stomach sinking—and then go to my bedroom and pull the blinds shut. A foul shiver swims up my arms and stitches its way back down my spine. Winter's letter swims through my brain. That...*thing* in the park changed me. I've suspected it for a while now, the way my shadow wavers and curls in the sun, the motion unnatural, like it's moving on its own. And indoors, how it slides over the walls like a flicker of smoke when touched by the lamplight.

I close my eyes and let the last line crash through my head like a thunderstorm.

Kyle, I'm so sorry, but whatever you do, you must never, ever go outside.

YOU ALWAYS WANTED A GARDEN

You always wanted a garden. Nothing big, mind you, just a bed out back with enough room for some carrots and snow peas, and a stalk or two of corn. You talked about it all the time—how you spent your childhood elbow-to-elbow with your mother, digging in the soil of your youth. You wanted to do the same with our son, to teach him the simple joys of hard work and spending time with those you love. You imagined the look on his face as he bit into the first sun-warmed strawberry of the season, the way he'd smile.

It wasn't a big ask, your garden. I wanted it, too, but life got in the way. A doctor appointment here, a flat tire there. A trip to the vet with Spot when Brandon fed him all those vitamins. Something always seemed more pressing. Eventually, it became our inside joke. I'd ask to go on a hunting trip with the guys or spend the weekend fly fishing, and you'd say, *Sure, just as soon as you finish that garden.* We'd share a laugh, and then you'd smirk and roll your eyes at the door. *Go on, get out of here.*

A week after Brandon turned six, I decided to surprise you. You'd be back from your jog any minute, I told him. We'd need to hurry. He was so excited as we unloaded the boards for the planter from the truck and covered them in the checkered tablecloth you brought on picnics. I set a bottle of your favorite pinot on top, along with two wine glasses, and pictured how your eyebrows would rise when you returned from your run.

You never came home. Another jogger found you collapsed beneath a strand of bur oak with your eyes wide open. An atrial septal defect, your doctor told me. A hole in your heart...one neither of us knew was there.

Your parents wanted to bury you, but I wouldn't let them. You'd made me promise as much, that night we spent in the Catskills staring at the stars. It was a beautiful thing to return to nature, you said. The cycle of life: Ashes to ashes. Dust to dust. All of that.

It took a year before I gathered the courage to move the pile of wood and mulch and heavy plastic sheeting to the backyard. The HOA wrote me letter after letter. *Move it, or we'll fine you. We'll put a lien on your house.* I couldn't. I fell apart every time I tried. Whenever I looked at it, all I could think about was you. About how I'd *failed* you. You were everything to me, and I put everything else first.

I started on your garden today. Brandon helped. You should have seen the way his eyes lit up when we finished the box, the way he bit his lower lip and tugged on his ear. He reminded me so much of you at that moment. It made me wonder if you were there, hidden somewhere inside of him, looking back at me with your mannerisms baked into the coils and strands of his DNA.

"It's just like Momma always wanted! Don't you think?"

"Uh-huh." I kept my gaze low as I raked the soil. I didn't want him to see my tears.

It's been a month, and nothing will grow. Even the tomato vines I brought home from the nursery are wilting. I checked the pH. I scattered the limestone and sulfur just like the blue-haired woman in the checkout line told me to, with a hand spreader carefully measured out in cups. I installed drip lines and a pole with a fake owl perched on top to make sure the rabbits wouldn't get at the seeds. Nothing worked.

It's like the earth is poisoned. Like it knows all of this is much too late.

I brought you with me this morning. I carried you to the garden along with an Adirondack and sat there staring at all that empty brown soil. I held you in my lap, in the only urn I'd been able to find that seemed to suit you—a light blue cornflower ceramic stamped in doves. Something about the color reminded me of Miller Pond where I saw you for the first time, sitting on the bench next to the water. When I asked what you were reading, you told me, but I didn't hear a word. I was lost in the way you tilted your head, in the way you smiled. I loved that smile—it was like you were giving me a little peek at the sun.

It's become a ritual, this thing. Just you and me, sitting in our chair beside your garden. I sip my coffee and we talk. Sometimes about the weather. Sometimes about other things, like the way I can't seem to function at work anymore or keep the house organized. How, these days, I drink more than I should. But mostly I talk about Brandon. He's broken without you here. There's no light left in his eyes. He seems older than six, and sadder by far; sadder than a child his age has any right to be. He needs you now more than ever, and all I have to give him is me.

It's not nearly enough.

We spread your ashes this evening. I hadn't planned to—it just happened. We were outside, you and me, watching the sunset when Brandon tugged on my sleeve.

"Can I hold Momma?"

"Sure, but be gentle," I told him.

He cradled you in his arms like a baby and looked at you like he was holding his heart. I knew then he would never heal with you here. He would never move on.

We poured you into the garden together, just the two of us, watched you mix with all that dark, rich earth.

"She'll love it here," Brandon whispered when we were done. "I just know she will."

And when he said it, I knew he was right.

"Daddy, quick, come look. Something's growing!"

Brandon said it the next morning, standing in the kitchen doorway with his cheeks puffing red. And something *was* growing, but not what I'd expected. No peppers budding green. No fruit taking shape. It was something…else. An elegant, olive-green vine twined around a pole, thick with bunches of creamy white blooms. It didn't make sense for something like that to grow overnight. It was too fully formed, too exquisite. I stared at it for hours. I swore I saw it move.

Over the next several days, you took shape. Your torso formed first, followed by a face of intricately woven stems. I watched in wonder as your ocean-colored eyes flowered beneath a mane of mandarin blossoms. Then came your cheekbones, perfectly delicate, your ears and jaw and neck. It left me breathless.

I slept outside. At times, it was hard to see you through my tears, but I could smell you. Taste you. Lavender and mint, and something close to honey. Your hands formed last, your fingers reaching for me, extending in a way that made me want to take them in mine. But I couldn't. I was afraid you'd fall apart at my touch.

Brandon took them instead.

He slipped past while I slept. I never heard a sound. When I woke, there wasn't much human left of him...only a few slivers of freckle-covered skin peeking out from among all the vines. His fingers were out and reaching toward me in a mirror of yours, his lips curved in a cherry-blossom smile. He looked happy in a way I hadn't seen since the day you died. He looked at peace.

I sat there all day, in my chair, staring at the two of you, wondering if I had the strength to take your hand. What would happen? What would I become? You offered no answers save for a look, your eyes as blue as the day you died, formed in petals, your mouth outlined in pale pink buds.

At dusk, I stood and gazed out at the pastel sky, at the mountains beneath, glowing on the horizon in warm purple imprints. I wasn't sure I'd ever seen a sight so stunning. And I never wanted to again, I decided, unless it was with you.

So, it was with a full heart that I reached out—and took your hand.

THE BACKWARD MAN

Most of my childhood memories are like charcoal drawings, with the edges frayed, the images smudged and bleeding. But not this one. Not him.

The first time I saw the Backward Man, I was seven. It was spring. Mom and I were waiting at a stoplight, and I happened to glance up as the walk signal changed. There he was, standing on the other side of the street with his back to me, his top hat nearly scraping the traffic light. I remember pointing him out as we crossed, saying something like, "Look, Mom...look how tall that man is."

And she did, stopping just long enough to tilt her head at him before a car horn blared. What happened next seared my brain like a high-voltage camera flash:

Me flying into empty air.

The crunch of bone somewhere behind me.

Asphalt biting my skin and my body rolling.

Rolling, rolling...

Blood in my mouth and my eyes, my fingers a broken, mangled mess. And I'm bawling with these huge, gulping sobs crawling up my throat.

Mommy!

I spotted her a few feet away, lying on the street with her soft yellow sundress spattered red. I remember looking at her belly, which was tight with my baby brother Jake at the time, and knowing she was just...gone. That she'd left the two of us behind to fend for ourselves.

And beyond her, the Backward Man, standing so incredibly tall in his pitch-black suit and ragged top hat. My tears blurring him away.

The Backward Man appeared every so often after that. Maybe once a year. Twice. Sometimes more, sometimes less. Every time, though, it was as if he were some sort of silent, blaring alarm—this harbinger of doom only I could see. Could *feel...* prickly sensations like a swarm of centipedes racing down my legs. A heavy, tensing weight in my gut.

The hair on my arms would rise, I'd look up, and there he'd be. Always standing backward, always dressed in his tattered frock coat and black wool trousers. Everything about him terrified me. The pink slice of scalp beneath his top hat, so shiny and moist. The pencil-thin legs and shoulder blades that looked sharp enough to cut through his jacket. And the way he simply stood there, facing away, never once looking back. It bothered me.

But that wasn't the worst part. No, the worst part always came after I saw him.

There were more car wrecks. One so bad that four teenagers died on the spot. Dad was there for that one, hustling me away, doing his best to shield my eyes with his hands. It didn't matter. I saw most of it. The flickers of broken bodies trapped inside a pile of warped metal, and the Backward Man perched beyond the carnage—a skeleton in a suit dancing in the heatwaves.

The image haunted me for weeks, the nightmares for far longer.

It went on like that for years. The death of my sweet boxer, Buck, poisoned by a loaf of bread drenched in antifreeze. My aunt Debby's breast cancer, the Backward Man painting a cold shadow outside my bedroom window as Dad took the call: *Uh-huh. I see. Okay. We'll be right there.*

I told Dad about the Backward Man a few times. He'd nod and pretend to listen, steepling his fingers like he was paying attention, but he wasn't. Not really. He chalked my stories up to trauma from Mom's death, said I'd hit my head too hard that day. That, and he was only ever half-there, anyway. After Mom died, his eyes emptied, the *Vacancy* sign always blinking. I'm pretty sure the only thing that kept him going was me and my brother.

Especially my brother.

At first, he treated Jake like this fragile piece of Mom that God had somehow saved. This NICU miracle draped in IV lines. A reason for him to get up in the morning. A sliver of purpose, as fleeting as it was. But it didn't last. Mom's death had ruined him. Hollowed him out. Something in his gaze reminded me of a TV show bleeding static.

We were out in the Cascades when I discovered the Backward Man didn't like fire. It was just me and Jake and Dad camped next to a green stretch of mountain forest. The sun had nearly set, the air going heavy with the scent of earth and pitch, when that familiar tingle burned up my spine.

It took a moment, but I spotted him tucked away, standing in a gray-blue strand of fir. His frame was more shadow than light, his torso blotting out what remained of the day. I remember staring at him, mouth dry, as he edged from the forest, walking backward in this sick lumbering gait with his knees buckled in reverse. *Snap, crunch. Snap, crunch.* I'd never seen him move before. Not once. And it terrified me.

I opened my mouth to cry out as he drew closer, to tell Dad, *Watch out! He's right behind you!* but my voice lodged itself in the small part of my throat. All I could do was watch him approach with his shoulders rolled back against his coat, his neck crystalizing into a swirl of scarred, pink flesh. Then, Dad lit the campfire, and the Backward Man simply vanished.

"Earth to Colin," Dad said, clapping at me a moment later. "You with us?"

And just like that, I was, the crisp tinge of smoke and pine seeping into my lungs and reminding me to breathe again. I looked at the fire and knew what it meant.

I'd finally found a weapon.

We moved to Seattle when I was a freshman in high school, Jake in third grade. Dad had landed a supervisor position at some meatpacking plant in the city and thought a fresh start was what we needed to get over Mom. What *he* needed. It wasn't. All that cloud cover only drove him deeper into the bottle. Most nights, he stayed out way too late and forgot to make us breakfast the next morning. He stopped doing the laundry and stocking the fridge. You know, the basic stuff.

I'm not going to lie—it was hard watching him deteriorate like that. Jake became my responsibility. I mean, we'd gotten along okay over the years, but I resented having to care for him full time. What about me? When would I ever get a chance to be a teenager? To sleep late on the weekends and party with my friends? Never, apparently. And even if I could, it would mean towing my eight-year-old kid brother along with me. Not cool.

Still, I bucked up and got it done. Jake was a good kid, bushy-tailed and all of that, with the best parts of Mom: her half-curve smile and the eyes like beach water. He had her sense of humor, too. He was always laughing, spouting off one dumb joke after another: *Whaddaya call a cow that eats your grass? A lawn moo-er.* Ha, ha, ha.

But as much as he clowned around pretending to be a kid, I could see the pain in his eyes, the hurt Dad's drinking caused. There were questions there, baked into the way he stared at a father and son tossing a football in the park or casting fishing lines across a slice of sun-drenched river.

Why doesn't he love me like that, Colin? What did I do?

I couldn't tell him it wasn't what he did, but rather who he was. All Dad saw when he looked at Jake was Mom.

It was late one night, Dad out on another one of his benders, when I decided Jake was due for some fun. We weren't supposed to just up and leave, but I was sick of Dad's shit and Jake seemed down, so off we went. We hit up the mall, had burgers and shakes, and joked around like we were normal kids with normal lives, never mind all the other normal kids with normal lives eating dinner all around us with their normal parents. Jake didn't notice, though—he was too busy dipping his fries in his shake and laughing at my jokes. I didn't eat much, myself; I just sat there and watched him smile.

When we finally stumbled into the alley a couple of hours later, it was well past eleven and a thick bank of fog had rolled in. We were cracking up about how Jake had trounced some kid in a game of air hockey, nothing remotely scary on our mind, when the cramp rolled up my leg. That sinister tingle I'd hoped to never feel again.

At first, I thought the shadow was a weird trick of the light. A distortion. The fog did that sometimes—warped things, made them look sinister when they weren't—but then the shadow straightened, and I knew.

I shot an arm out to stop Jake, but he'd already paused, was standing there pale-faced and unblinking.

"Jake, do you...do you see him, too?"

His answer came in the form of a wobble, and then he was marching straight down the alley toward the Backward Man. I panicked. I snatched a Zippo from my pocket, and bolted past him, flicking the spark wheel like a maniac, as fast as I could, until the blue flame crackled and leaped from the wick. I held it aloft.

And the Backward Man did...nothing.

He just stood there facing away with his top hat corked to one side, a gluey ribbon of scalp peeking out from beneath the brim. Then, he was backing straight toward me with his knees popping, his joints grinding in a way that made it sound like they'd been packed with broken glass.

I glanced back at Jake, who'd stopped directly behind me and was staring right through me—I mean, *straight fucking through*—with a string of drool leaking off his lip. That's when

I spotted the stack of cardboard and old newspaper piled against the brick a few feet to his left. I rushed for it and brought the flame low and held it there until the pile caught.

When I looked up again, the Backward Man was gone.

I only asked Jake about that night once, a week later. His forehead buckled when I did. *Backward who?* I let it drop after that. If he didn't remember, that was a good thing...not that it made any sense. I mean, I couldn't forget it, so how could he?

Still, the fact that Jake had seen him at all bothered me. And the look he'd had in the alley with that zombie shuffle and the glassy eyes, what was that all about? In a way, Jake's behavior made me wonder if the Backward Man had been there for him instead of me. It was a question to which I didn't want an answer.

But it came anyway.

August. The summer had been unbearably hot with blankets of humidity blowing off the Sound for weeks. To top things off, the A/C was broken, and Dad hadn't bothered to fix it (like so many other things in the house) so I'd taken to sleeping with my window open.

I'm not exactly sure what woke me. Maybe the wind ruffling the dogwoods at the edge of our lawn, or the moonlight washing through the blinds. Whatever the cause, I snapped awake like I was in the middle of a horror movie. I mean, I just sat straight up in bed, sheened in sweat, with this awful smell clouding the air. Imagine an abandoned slaughterhouse left to bake in deep summer. Miles of spoiled meat.

Yeah, worse than that.

I bolted to my feet and crept to the window. Sure enough, there he was, partially obscured by a dense bank of lilacs, his frock coat billowing in the breeze. He looked like something a child might sketch, bathed in all that buttery moonlight. A stick-figure drawing of the Bogeyman, but so, *so* much worse. And ten yards away was Jake, walking straight for him.

I snatched my Zippo and was about to hurdle over the window-sill when the memory of the alley surfaced. The lighter wouldn't cut it. I reversed course and pounded for the garage, threw on the light, and scoured the space for the gas can. I found it buried beneath Dad's workbench and grabbed it along with a wad of paper towels, then sprinted into the backyard and stopped cold.

The Backward Man had knelt, his arms slung out in reverse as if to beckon Jake closer for some perverse hug. His arms cut impossible angles, the elbows inverted in a way that made my stomach hurt.

I burst across the grass while uncapping the gas can. Several paper towels fluttered from my grip, but I managed to jam most of them into the spout before sliding in front of Jake. I flicked the lighter and had brought the flame down to light a paper towel when Jake thudded into my back. The gas can and the lighter tumbled from my grip, and the flame sputtered out instantly.

The Backward Man rose, uncoiling into an impossibly black shadow against a cold slab of moonlight. His skin rippled with a familiar motion that took me a second to place—something like bubbles rising through his flesh. Like his flesh was...*boiling,* blackening as he edged closer to us, with tendrils of ash coiling off his fingers.

That's what saved us…a single spark arcing from his wrist as it cracked with heat lines. It wavered there, hung like a firefly for a terrible moment, winking in and out, before finally settling into the pool of gas, glug-glugging toward the Backward Man's feet. A hot *whoosh!* sent branches of flame racing up his legs toward his waist.

I'd like to say the Backward Man screamed, but the sound he emitted was something else entirely. A piercing cry like he'd been thrust into the middle of an interstate pileup with a thousand brakes screeching at once. This awful metallic squeal that dropped me to my knees and forced my hands to my ears.

I felt like it continued for an eternity, but in reality probably only went on for a few seconds. Either way, it was long enough to leave my palms streaked in blood. The same thing happened to Jake. Dark fingers of blood were leaking down his neck when he pulled his hands from his ears. He blinked hard and tried to focus, rubbed his eyes.

"What are we doing out here?"

He asked the question as if I could somehow answer it. I couldn't. All I knew was that I would do whatever it took to protect him, to make sure the Backward Man never hurt him again.

I moved my mattress into Jake's room after that. Slept next to the window and kept his door locked. Dad thought I was nuts and tried to get me to go back to my room, but finally conceded with a weary, "I guess it doesn't hurt anything."

Jake, on the other hand, loved it.

We played video games until midnight and talked more than we ever had before. Sports. Girls. Movies. What he wanted to be when he grew up. An astronaut or a pilot. When he fell asleep, I forced myself to stare out his window until my eyelids turned to concrete.

Never again, I promised.

"Colin," Jake said one night as we laid there, both of us looking up at the ceiling, "what was she like?"

"Who, Mom?"

"Yeah."

I tried to picture her. She'd gone blurry in my mind—now mostly a cascade of chestnut hair and a featureless face. "I don't remember much, buddy," I said. "I was pretty young when she passed. But I can remember this: she loved me. And you, too. Especially you. She was so excited to meet you."

He was silent for a moment, his mouth bunching into a wistful twist. "Me, too."

A few years passed without incident. Jake grew up and fell into theater, acted in a few plays, and began painting—another piece of Mom surfacing. Her work still hung in our living room. Portraits of lush summer skies at sunset. Bright fields of cornflowers and aspens in full fall blaze. My favorite hung near the front door: a beachside seascape of Mom and me with Dad standing on the other side wearing a candy-red raincoat, all of us looking out at the break.

It hurt Dad, that painting, but he couldn't bear to take it down. I sometimes caught him staring at it late at night, breaking on the inside with a beer hanging limp in his hand, no clue that I was right there breaking with him.

Besides that, things were pretty normal…just not enough so to blot out the memory of the night Jake slogged across the lawn toward the Backward Man like some back-alley drunk. Nothing could erase that. And as much as I wanted to ignore the thought, to bury it in some far corner of my brain, I knew he'd be back. So, I did the only thing I could.

I prepared.

It's amazing what you can find on the dark web if you're dedicated enough. It's a bad place full of awful shit just like everyone says—drugs and stolen credit cards and extremist agendas. Lots of weird and illegal porn, too...crap I wanted nothing to do with. What I was looking for were instructions on how to build a kick-ass Molotov cocktail.

Finding the right recipe took a while, along with a lot of experimenting and several burns, one a second-degree scorcher that consumed most of my wrist. It was worth it, though. In the end, I settled on a highly illegal mix of carbon disulfide, white phosphorus, and sulfur. Something that would ignite on contact with oxygen. I could avoid the messy ignition rags that way, and even better, there was no smell, which meant there was no way anyone could tell I was carting a couple of firebombs around in my backpack.

Jake was a high school freshman by then. He seemed fine. Mostly normal, or as normal as any high school kid can seem. Part of me wanted to ease up a bit and enjoy my life. I mean, I'd sacrificed college to protect the kid, including taking a crap job down at the Grease Monkey on the corner just to help Dad pay the bills.

He's not coming back, I told myself. *He's gone for good.*

But I knew the Backward Man wasn't gone—could somehow feel it in my gut—and the image of Jake consumed by all that boiling flesh without me there to watch over him scared the hell out of me. So, I doubled down and did the opposite; I smothered him. I coached his soccer teams and took him to art lessons. I drove him anywhere he needed to go. Doctor appointments and study dates. Trips to friends' houses...all that crap. And I still slept in his room, even when he begged me not to, all the while waiting for the Backward Man to return.

It wasn't until December of his freshman year that I slipped up. Jake had landed the lead in some play set during the Civil War. I vaguely remember the irritation I felt when he told me, face beaming. I forced a smile to cover the cringe inside. The play meant more time spent carting him around—more time I needed to carve from my already bursting-at-the-seams schedule. Still, I knew how much the kid loved acting, so I congratulated him and told myself to buck up.

I didn't realize how big of a deal the play was until opening night. It seemed like the entire school had turned out, everyone stuffed into tightly packed rows. The place buzzed with body heat. Even Dad was there—sober for once, and stretched out next to me looking half-interested.

The first scene was a battle, the North versus the South, complete with fog machine theatrics and the snap of cap gun rifles. Everything seemed to go off without a hitch. So much so that I found myself enjoying it. The kids barked out their lines with gusto, looking the part in their period-perfect costumes.

It wasn't until the third act that my stomach began to churn. Jake had taken the stage for his big scene, the one he'd practiced in front of the mirror for months. The Gettysburg Address. He stood hunched, with his fake beard plastered to his chin and his body stiff beneath a knock-off, double-breasted suit. I could tell he was nervous by the way he rocked back on his heels and clutched the podium. For a moment, I thought he'd forgotten his lines, but then he straightened and cleared his throat.

"Fourscore and seven years ago..."

I don't think I'd ever been as proud of him as I was at that moment. Same with Dad. He was grinning cheek-to-cheek. He somehow looked younger, fresher, the creases in his face seeming to fill in.

That's when I saw the shadow.

It started as a slight alteration in the way the light hit the stage...muted in spots, hazy, almost like the impending aura of a migraine.

Is it really there? Am I actually seeing this?

I was. It spread over the floor behind Jake inch by horrible inch. A top hat forming. A sharp set of clavicles and a spindly neck. I reached for my backpack and clawed empty air.

No.

I'd carried it around like an oxygen tank, day in and day out, for over a year, waiting for this moment—this *exact* moment—and, like an idiot, had left it in the car when I'd dropped Jake off earlier.

I bolted from the seat and shoved my way through a tangle of legs—*Go! Go! Go!*—and into the hall. By the time I made it back to the auditorium, Jake had deteriorated, with the play director hissing lines at him through an otherwise awkward silence.

"It is altogether fitting! Altogether fitting!"

Jake had turned to face the Backward Man with his head lolled at an awkward angle. The other kids onstage watched him with furrowed brows, one a popular, pony-tailed sophomore doing her best to stifle a nervous shot of laughter. I could tell she didn't see the Backward Man.

No one did. No one but Jake.

The Backward Man elongated, his top hat nearly brushing the stage lights, and beckoned for Jake to come closer. Jake gurgled something and wobbled off the podium toward him. A sound like a teakettle moaning lit the air as I ran down the aisle and clambered up onto the stage. I flung the first Molotov, and it went wide right, shattering in a searing burst of light. Someone in the audience screamed. I focused and hurled the second Molotov harder. *Do not miss, Colin, don't you fucking miss.*

It all happened at once. Jake reaching out for those horrible hands. The Molotov exploding in a bright wall of flame that enveloped the curtains and bled over Backward Man.

Jake.

I was only vaguely aware of the hell breaking loose behind me, of the shrieks and frantic surge for the exits.

I lunged for Jake's arm. His mouth unbuckled in a silent scream, all teeth. Then, that shrill cry hit—the terrible metal-on-metal wail of the Backward Man—and I was pulling, heaving back on Jake like a man possessed, wailing for the Backward Man to, "Please, God! Please just let go!"

But he didn't. The Backward Man's grip was steel. *Stronger* than steel. He held Jake there with orange tongues of flame spreading from his arm to my brother's, his head rotating toward me like the girl from *The Exorcist*. The eyes appeared first, followed by a familiar fringe of hair.

His mouth hung open in a scream, and my world fell away.

It was...*Jake*. A funhouse mirror version of him, but him all the same, and so, so *wrong*. His cheeks were hollowed out and slung in paste-like ribbons of flesh. His eyes bulged, one rolling wildly in place, the other staring directly at me with a pupil drowning in a sea of yellowed sclera. And his nose, if you could call it that, was nothing more than two gaping holes in the place of nostrils. I realized then that the Backward Man was crying, as was Jake, both of them howling as the flames chewed into their torsos and bled down their legs.

My hand fell away, and all I can remember is shaking, convulsing in place as the Backward Man congealed with Jake, the two of them melting into one another, becoming one another in this awful *combining*. I have no other word for it.

A twining of arms. A melding of legs and necks and hips and feet.

I saw it, then, what I should have seen all along: the top hats and frock coats billowing with smoke. The diamond-point bow ties and wool trousers.

Everything the same.

Their ankle boots. Their beards. Even their postures, both slumped slightly forward. They were the same. Exactly the same.

The flames expanded, bleeding over the floor and up my jeans. I didn't move. I just stood there with my nerve endings frying, watching my brother and this thing that was also my brother seizing together, the two of them convulsing and shrieking. I realized I was screaming, too, and had been for some time. Echoing the howls of Jake. Of the Backward Man.

Hands gripped my shoulders. A towel beat at my legs. I extended an arm toward what was left of Jake, his eyes never leaving mine until they merged with those of the Backward Man's. And then I was dragged away.

My legs aren't much to look at these days. I avoid mirrors whenever I can. All that twisted, candle-wax flesh brings me shrieking right back to the day Jake died. I don't need the reminder. I live it on repeat, the way he just dissolved into the Backward Man playing again and again in my mind. The memory is enough to make me want to shoot myself.

And I would if I could. But I can't. I was committed not too long after the fire, sentenced to twenty years in the psychiatric wing of King County Correctional. Fifteen with good behavior.

Maybe someday I'll make it to a halfway house where I can post up on a porch and chain-smoke my way through what's left of my meaningless life, but even that would be too kind. Fifteen people were hospitalized that night, including four students sent to the ICU with severe smoke inhalation. Two of them died—my brother and the girl I spotted giggling at him. I can still picture her blonde hair glowing pink beneath the stage lights and the way she swallowed that laugh when Jake lurched from the podium toward the Backward Man. Her parents were at my trial, their faces bunched in hate, fists balled hard in their laps. If eyes were bullets, I'd already be dead.

Dad never came to my hearings and hasn't visited me once in the ten years since. He's never written. Never called. If he did, I'd tell him what I've told everyone else: that I was just trying to protect Jake, to save him from the man in the frock coat that took Mom. It landed me here, that story, planted me in these sweat-yellowed scrubs along with the rest of the drooling psychopaths. Needless to say, no one else saw the Backward Man besides me and Jake that night. Not a single person.

Still, it doesn't change the fact that it's true. Every word.

Or is it? Maybe I *am* crazy. There's a good chance, I'll grant you that, but after a decade spent trying to work it out, to make sense of what I saw, here's what I've decided: the Backward Man was a warning. Death cloaked in a frock coat.

I should have taken Jake and run the second he burst into my room with his big news. *"Colin! I got the part! Can you believe it? I'm going to be Abraham Lincoln!"* It was all right there, staring me dead in the face...the image that had been burned into the nightmares of my youth. The same blackened figure in the top hat that I'd seen over, and over, and over again, throughout my entire life.

Jake was the Backward Man. The Backward Man was Jake.

And I didn't see it.

I'll pay for that mistake for the rest of my life. I'll relive that night every time I close my eyes and every morning when I open them, ready to choke down another day. Jake burning. Melting and coming apart. It's unbearable.

But I'll give you this. Despite how awful this place is with all the solitude, the thinly padded walls and the pipes clinking away in the small, dark hours, I'm not lonely. Not in the least. Jake is here with me. He stands in the corner with his top hat crushed beneath the ceiling. His eyes are always on me, never blinking, never looking at anything else. They remind me of two holes punched through a wet sheet of paper, pressed into a sheet of shining pink flesh.

Sometimes, his jaw elongates, and he tries to speak, but all that comes out is the shriek I know so well, that scraped-metal cry that sends a chill racing down my spine every time I hear it. I know that cry will never end. It will drill into my skull and fray my mind bit by bit. It will whittle me down to nothing more than a faded charcoal imprint until I wonder if I was ever really here at all.

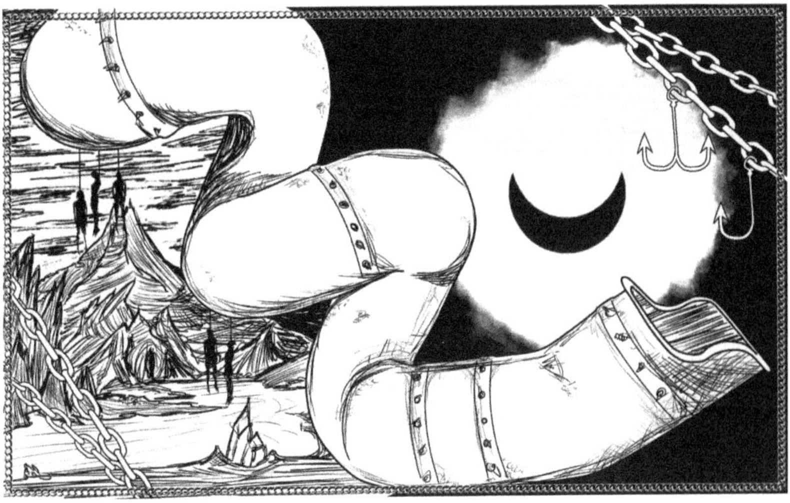

A SLIDE INFINITE

I'll never walk again. I knew it the moment I woke with the ambulance lights bleeding over my freshly broken body, Josh's head skewered on a tree limb next to me in the passenger seat. Mom says I'm the lucky one because I survived, and he didn't. I'm not so sure about that. Josh doesn't wake every night caked in sweat thinking his legs still work. Josh doesn't have to live with the *I know what you did* looks every time he leaves the house, or the crushing guilt that comes with killing your best friend.

But I'm not going to think about that today. No, today is about Lagoon Island and the twins. They've been begging Mom to bring them here all summer, begged and begged.

We're old enough to go, Mom! We're seven already.

You promised you would take us this year! You did too, Garret!

And I did. For years. Told them how much fun Devil's Drop was, bragged about the wave pool, and how I could body surf all that crashing water. They're out there in it right now with Mom, unleashing bright peals of laughter as she tosses them into the oncoming waves. I used to toss them like that. Make them laugh. That was my thing.

Now, I just sit here and watch.

And watch. And watch.

I groan and look away.

Their day, Garret, I chide myself. *Their—*

A glimmer of light catches my eye from across the pool, a shimmering distortion about the size of a door, situated next to Colonel Hook's snack shack. I wheel my way toward it, weaving through packs of screaming children and anxious parents who flow past me like I'm some giant, handicapped stone planted in the middle of a human river—which, of course, I am. Not that it matters. What *does* matter is that no one else is looking at the bizarre square of light. No one else seems to see it.

Not a single person except me.

I roll through the dense tangle of bodies a little faster, half-expecting the distortion to be gone when I break free from the crowd, but it's not. It's only grown stronger, brighter—this kaleidoscope of color that's so vibrant, so lush, the air is practically dripping with it. Waves of gooseflesh ripple over my arms as I wheel past the snack shack and over a dead patch of grass, the door close now, only a few feet away and—

"You okay, sweetheart?"

I startle and turn toward a woman wearing a floppy floral sunhat. Most of her face is cast in shadow, save for a bright pink ring of lipstick glowing with the force of a cheap neon beer sign.

She raises a hand. "Oh, I'm sorry. I didn't mean to frighten you."

"It's okay. I was just looking at..." I wave at the patch of swirling light. "At that."

She turns and plants a hand on her hip. "At what?"

She doesn't see it, either.

"Are you here with someone, dear?" she asks, swiveling back to me. "You look a little pale. Can I help you find anyone?"

I don't answer, just stare at the soapy mix of light and air roiling in front of me…and then I roll straight through.

To a waterslide.

I'm staring at a *waterslide.*

At least I think that's what it is—a gleaming crystal tube curling down through a slab of chipped concrete. Water chimes invitingly as it bubbles and rushes forward into the ground. It makes no sense and looks nothing like the other slides at Lagoon Island, with the brightly colored PVC long faded by the sun.

Lagoon Island.

I glance back at it, and a woozy rush of blood nearly tips me from my chair.

The woman in the floppy hat stands with her hands akimbo and her mouth propped open like she's still talking to me. Beyond her, a boy sprayed in freckles hangs suspended above a diving board like someone tacked him there with a giant hammer. And they're not alone. The water, the waves, the groups of people trapped in idle conversation—all of it, the entire park, is frozen in a crush of glistening skin.

I blink. Hard.

This can't be happening.

Maybe it's not. Maybe I'm stroked out on the concrete somewhere, foaming at the mouth and imagining it all, but I don't think so. It feels too…*real.* And this slide with no stairs to climb or handrails to navigate, no signs warning off the disabled—it looks like it was placed here just for me.

There's no easy way out of the chair. Nothing to grasp. All I can do is get as low to the cement as possible before thrusting forward, which I do without thinking, my legs smacking off the cement like the two numb and lifeless appendages they are. They no longer belong to me. They belong to the boy who came before the wheelchair, the one who thought he was invincible, could drive drunk whenever he wanted. *I'm fine, I promise.*

I roll over and sit up, then ease over the slide's lip. I know I should be more worried about this, terrified even, but I'm not. I'm excited, a swarm of butterflies ravaging my stomach, my nerves singing. Since the crash, my life has been a never-ending series of doctor appointments and surgeries interspersed with bouts of shame so sticky-thick it feels like someone bottled it up and then smeared it over my lungs until they could no longer absorb oxygen. For the last eighteen months, I haven't made a decision of my own. Not one. All I've done is rot in my wheelchair and *exist*…and even then, just barely.

And, here, right now, I want to—*need to*—know where this slide leads.

I thrust my hands into the water...and shove off.

The tube whips left, right, drops, and goes vertical, pulling my broken body into total darkness. Needles of water spray my face, my neck. A scream rips up my throat, only to die on my tongue; I'm moving so fast, I'm afraid the slide will peel the skin from my bones.

I go faster still, losing all sense of direction as I zoom around curve after endless curve, the speed flattening my cheeks and stretching my lips. I'm a human bullet careening through a never-ending chamber of black. I screw my eyes shut and clench my jaw so tight it feels like my molars will crack.

This was a mistake. A terrible, terrible mistake.

Seams of blinding light cut through my eyelids. I snap them open to blooms of luminescence swirling outside the tube as I rocket lower. Colors streak past me in contrails so intense they sear my retinas. Breathtaking blues and electric greens. Pale, cinnamon reds that sparkle like lazy Fourth of July fireworks. Glittering clouds of dust shimmer brilliantly around me in gem-like bunches that blossom and fade, only to blossom again; entire galaxies born and reborn.

I have no words to describe what I'm seeing. It's all so... *beautiful.*

The most beautiful thing I've ever seen.

And then it's gone, snatched away as the slide plunges into a throbbing crimson throat. A series of red lights pulse overhead as I race through another loop and begin to slow—slowing, slowing—until I'm spit into a slice of cold, dead air.

I hurtle from the slide and glimpse a stretch of water rushing upward so fast, I barely manage to take a breath before I slam into it. My chest constricts as the surface darkens above, cold liquid fingers wrapping around my chest and pulling me lower. I'm sinking, working my arms in frantic circles that do little to overcome the pillars of cement that are my legs dragging me down, down, down.

My lungs burn. My vision sparks and flickers. A thought races through my brain: this is how I'm going to die, alone and helpless, a broken, worthless corpse drowned at the bottom of the world with no one to—

My right quad twitches. Contracts.

My left.

I gasp and suck in a mouthful of frigid water as my legs come to life beneath me. My paralyzed, useless legs *moving*. It's all I can do to keep from screaming as I surge upward and burst through the surface.

Gulp air and blink.

I'm in a cavern of some sort. It's beyond immense—illuminated with cauldrons of flame that dangle overhead, chained to a smooth granite dome. On either side of me are more slides protruding from the same vertical sheet of rock from which I just emerged. Crystal tubes ejecting body after body, spitting them into the same liquid expanse I'm currently treading with legs that shouldn't be able to obey my commands to move.

Splash! Splash! Splash!

A scream splits the air, and a girl in a yellow bikini hurtles from the slide to my right. She flops hard into the water and swims toward a long stone bank across from the slides, one I hadn't noticed until now. I follow suit, pulling myself through the water with jumbled, flopping strokes until I'm kneeling on hard ground.

The girl heaves herself onto the stone and collapses onto her back, flexing her fingers in front of her face like she's never moved them before, like she's never once seen her hands. A man with a head full of dreadlocks rolls onto the ledge just beyond her, a look of wonder splashed across his face as he gapes open-mouthed at his legs and his feet. And not just him.

All of them.

Every single person down the line pulling themselves from the water and gawking at some part of their body like it's the first time they've seen it work.

Because it is, I realize. *They're broken just like me.*

"Welcome!"

The voice booms from above as, twenty yards in front of us, an elaborately wrought iron cage descends from the darkness. And in the cage is this...*thing*. I have no other word for it. Thick cords of muscle wind over its chest and arms, its skin a pale, mottled white. An angular head rests on its shoulders, split by a mouth jammed with anthracite teeth.

"Welcome, you who are broken. You who are weary and cast out!" A forked tongue darts over its lips as it studies all of us in turn. "Each of you has been chosen. Each of you remade and reborn by the pool of life." It spreads four sinewed arms. "This is but a taste of the life you once had. A glimmer of renewal. But alas, only one of you may keep this precious gift." The thing turns a slow circle in the cage. "The champion of the gauntlet!"

A thunderous roar ignites all around me, from every direction. For the first time, I notice the perfect curve of the chamber, the travertine columns, and the elaborate arches supporting rows of stadium seating packed with creatures covered in russet skin and shining scales. Monstrous visages that watch us with looks of hungry anticipation, thousands upon thousands of eyes burning at us through the gloom, all of them blowtorch bright.

"Fifteen of you have earned this honor," the thing continues. "Kings and queens all."

A cold line of sweat snakes across my forehead. I glance at the others, their faces smeared with panic, their eyes flicking between the creature and the crowd, wondering the same thing as me: *What the hell is happening?*

"Legion, I ask you this. Is salvation given?"

"No!" the crowd roars.

"Can it be bought?"

"No!"

"What then, I ask of you?"

"It must be earned!" a lone voice shrieks.

"Louder!"

A roar rises, the voices chanting as one: "Earned! Earned! Earned!"

The sound reverberates through the chamber and rattles my ribs.

The creature beats its chest and howls: "Competitors, behold your salvation!"

Four columns of fire ignite on the far side of the cavern, at least a football field's length away. A crystalline object glitters in response. It's a slide. A single, solitary slide, exactly like the one that brought me here, nothing between it and where we stand now but a blasted stretch of scorched rock.

The thing in the cage straightens to its full height and retrieves a giant, ornate horn from its belt. "Whoever reaches the slide first shall keep their gift. Fifteen must now become one." It lifts the horn to its lips. "Let the gauntlet...begin!"

The tone of the horn is unearthly, a terrible pressure that envelopes my head as the other competitors—are they competitors?—cover their ears. No one moves, save a woman in a purple bathing suit, who straightens and dashes forward first.

Go, a voice in my head blares. *Run, Garret!*

I do, awkwardly and with great effort, my new legs buckling beneath me after several wavering steps.

The fall is all that saves me.

A man barrels past on my left and impales himself on a series of metallic spikes that piston from the stone with a sudden *Clack!* Black fountains of blood pour from his back and legs. He convulses and slides down the spikes, which are now gleaming wet and red.

Time stops, and I forget to breathe.

I can't move, can't think.

An image tickles my brain.

I've seen this before: the concentric rings of flagstone and the marble notched with interlacing grooves. The crowd and the traps and the howling bloodlust. In history class, when we studied ancient Rome.

It hits me then, exactly where I am.

I'm in a coliseum and, *Jesus,* I'm one of the gladiators.

"C'mon! C'mon!" Hands seize my shoulders and pull me upright. "Let's go!"

The girl in the bikini. Already moving, dashing away in front of me.

I lurch after her and grab her forearm as a blade the size of a tractor tire whirs past so close I feel it pass in a rush of wind. The man next to us isn't so lucky. It cleaves him in half, foot to neck, along with two others who peel apart in shining slabs of intestine and muscle that slop to the rock.

Holy fuck.

A dark-haired woman scrambles between them, only to be incinerated by a wall of flame.

The crowd roars.

We run, weaving past more of the pistoning spikes, and evade yet another blade that eviscerates the guy with the dreads before a deep vibration brings us to a stop. I search for its source and count six...no, *seven* other competitors still standing, all of them looking around wildly, wondering where it's coming from.

The grinding stops. We're halfway to the slide.

A man in jean shorts bolts forward and makes it five feet before a granite column surges from the ground beneath his feet and launches him headfirst into the crowd. The creatures there scatter then creep back with extruded tongues and lips pulled wide in keening howls. His screams are the stuff of nightmares as they tear him apart.

I look back in time to see another granite column surge toward the cavern dome. And another, column after column sheering higher until they form a narrow canyon of polished stone.

"Behold the Bloody Gorge!" the beast above bellows.

Beyond it, the slide shines like a lighthouse in the middle of a gale, the beam beckoning us forward. There's no other way to reach it but through.

The creatures come to their feet with their clawed fists pumping—horrible, scaled appendages that flash in time with their guttural chant: "Gorge! Gorge! Gorge!"

I take the girl's hand and yank her toward the crevice. She resists and pulls me back, her face bleach white. "No, hold on!" she says, nodding at the others. "There have to be more traps. Let them go first and show us where they are."

It's a good idea.

We don't have to wait long. The woman in the purple swimsuit races for the gap, followed by a kid who's about the twins' age. After that, it's chaos, everyone surging forward in a melee of elbows and knees as they pour into the canyon.

"Now!" the girl shouts.

We fly into the crevice. The woman is already too far in front of us, leaping from side to side, when a sharp click cleaves the air. A stone buttress rockets sideways from one wall and catches her mid-rib before pounding her into the far wall in a moist crunch.

The girl yelps.

"Don't look!" I tell her, choking back a slug of bile as the click echoes again. Another colossal boom of stone rocks the walls, two more bodies turned into shapeless piles of grizzle sliding down the sheer granite face.

Five competitors left.

Run.

We sprint onward. A white-hot splinter of pain pierces my heel. It burns, blood seeping from the wound and turning the rock beneath me slick. But I don't stop. *Don't you dare stop, Garret.* Ahead, two men repeat the same side-to-side leaping motion as the woman before a blast of steam incinerates the one on the right.

I soon see why. The floor is honeycombed in front of us, with three-foot-wide alternating marble panels offsetting empty stretches of air. Black clouds of sulfur belch through the gaps, a river of lava flowing twenty feet beneath them, its surface bisected in glowing skeins of orange and red molten rock.

I look at the girl. "We have to jump!"

A hawk-faced woman bolts between us as I say it and leaps without hesitation, landing awkwardly on one of the panels before jumping to the next. The boy I spotted earlier, the one close to the twins' age, pulls level with us and gazes down from the edge at the boiling magma with his mouth split wide in a rictus of fear.

"I can't make it across that!"

His chin quivers, and for a moment, I see Alex standing next to me, alone and helpless, my little brother staring down into a flaming morass he can never hope to cross alone.

He takes a step back, and I open my mouth to call out to him, to tell him I'll help him through this, that I'll get him home, wherever his home is, when a flurry of steel-tipped bolts spit from the wall and send him rag-dolling forward through one of the gaps.

No. My muscles feel like they'll slough off my bones.

The voice from above thunders down. "Make haste, competitors. Those who linger will be dealt with unfavorably."

"Go!" the girl squeals, raking my arm with her fingernails. "Go! Go! Go!"

I jump and land on a marble panel, push off and leap for the next, praying my legs won't fail me, that they'll have the strength to propel me across. Hot steam whooshes past me, the smell of acrid heat filling my nostrils and coating my tongue. I leap again and again, the girl leaping with me until we're both safe on the other side, breathing hard, the girl's face streaked in ash.

We scramble on.

Ahead, the buttresses explode across the gorge, only there are no bodies this time. No fresh piles of human gruel shivering down the stone, save those already crushed. Instead, I see two figures working their way through the horizontal stone beams as they retract back into position—the woman who passed us a moment ago and a bald man wielding a pair of skeletal arms.

They must have found a way to trigger the trap.

"Hurry!" I tell the girl.

We race after them, past the beams, and sprint for the far edge of the crevasse. The man nears the edge of the chasm and unleashes a cry of delight, the woman running close behind.

Beyond them, twenty yards away, lies the slide.

I grab the girl's hand and pump my newly restored legs as fast as they'll go, begging them to go faster yet, the creature's words ripping through my mind like branches of lightning. *Fifteen must now become one.* Only one of us can make it to the slide. Only one.

We barrel past sharp pillars of rock and leap over piles of scree, the girl gasping next to me, trying to keep up. My heel is so slick with blood I can barely maintain my balance.

The man shoulders past the woman and bursts from the gorge in a mad dash for the slide.

He's close. *Too* close. We'll never reach him before—

"Release the bestia!"

A broad travertine slab disintegrates beneath the man's feet, and he tumbles into the resulting pit with a sharp cry. Something howls in response. It's a roar unlike anything I've ever heard—the sound of a thousand shrieking voices melted into one.

The man's cries turn wet and raw.

From the pit, a monstrosity appears. A nightmare with ivory horns jutting from a body layered in gleaming obsidian scales. It's beyond colossal, looking like a black widow mated with a bulldozer as it emerges on six multi-jointed legs. Its faceted, jewel-like eyes shine as if lit with some terrible internal torch, and in its maw are the remains of the man: a sliver of scalp and a spray of shattered limbs that disappear with a final, meaty crunch.

Dear God...

A blanket of silence falls over the arena, only three of us left now. Me, the girl, and the hawk-faced woman.

There's no sound. No motion.

I take the girl's hand, and we press back against the canyon wall.

The thing rotates its head with a guttural growl. Snorts. Its demon-like eyes devour the coliseum. I don't move. Don't breathe. The girl is shaking so hard next to me that I'm afraid she'll come apart. On the other side of the gorge, the woman crouches behind a shattered stone column, her eyes darting between us and the slide like a schizophrenic set of pinballs.

The beast snorts again and raises its head, firelight dancing over its horns and glossing its armor. It unleashes a haunting shriek, and a murmur of excitement ripples through the crowd. They can already taste the blood.

Our blood.

It eases closer, and a wave of panic sheets through my chest. I can smell the hot rot of its breath. Taste the death hanging in the air. I nudge the girl and nod at the slide. She shakes her head. Her face is paralyzed with fear, her eyes wide and wild. I squeeze her hand and will her to understand: *If we run, maybe one of us makes it. If we stay here, we die.*

And I don't want to die.

The woman moves first, a shadow bolting across the floor.

She's fast.

The beast is faster.

It rotates in one smooth motion and shortens the distance between them with horrifying speed. She leaps for the slide, and it snatches her mid-air. Gives her a shake. Her bones snap like gunshots.

A voice blares inside my head: *Now!*

I shove the girl forward, and we're moving, racing toward the slide behind the creature as it whips the woman back and forth. It's a sound like fabric tearing as she comes apart, a collection of moist weight splattering across a hard surface.

My feet smack off the stone, my heart expanding further with each step.

Ten feet to the slide.

Eight.

The beast still lapping entrails from the stone: *It doesn't see us.*

Six feet.

The crowd goes ballistic and wails for it to turn around, pointing at us in a forest of sharp, segmented figures. Screaming words I can't understand.

Four feet.

Two.

And then it sees us.

I hit the slide first. The girl lands beside me, and the water takes hold, both of us skimming forward. The slide rushing, pulling.

We made it! We both—

The girl jerks to a stop.

It's all I can do to reach back and seize her leg before the tube swallows me. She's shrieking, wailing for me to save her, to keep her safe. The beast has her by the arm, sending thick gouts of blood dripping off her elbow, turning the water around me to rust.

"Don't let go!" I shout at her. "Look at me! Hold on!"

She does, her face wracked with pain, her eyes burning in two pale beacons of panic.

I tighten my grip, but her hand slips an inch. Water spills past my head and tears at my feet. Then, the creature snaps forward, and the rest of her arm disappears into a sea of shining teeth.

"Champion!" a voice booms.

She cries out as her fingers slip from mine.

I fly from the slide and flop into a swimming pool. There's a scatter of motion, arcs of light wheeling my way as I swim to the ledge. A man in a Lagoon Island uniform waits to help me from the pool.

"He's over here!"

More workers rush our way as the man heaves me up and onto the cement. I ignore them and glance back for the slide, which is gone. *Was it ever there?* A dull ache floods my chest.

"Garret...oh my God." I turn around and spot Mom breaking through the crowd. "You're standing."

I look down at my legs and nod dumbly.

Yes. Yes, I am.

With a sob, she crashes into me. The twins wrap themselves around my waist a moment later, both of them shouting my name. "Garret! Garret! Garret!"

Mom reaches up and cups my cheeks with both hands, her eyes wet and shining. "How did this happen, Garret? *How?*"

I can't answer, and even if I could, she wouldn't believe me. Luckily, I don't have to. The man in the uniform takes me by the shoulder and guides me toward my wheelchair, which is sitting right next to the snack shack where I left it. But unlike this morning, there's no slide, only bare dirt and grass.

He directs me to sit and then crouches down to assess my foot. Over his shoulder, the sky is nearing dusk, streaked in layers of peach and deep blood orange.

He slaps a bandage on my heel and gives it a pat. "You'll probably want to get that checked out, buddy. Looks like it might need some stitches."

Mom assures him that, yes, of course, we'll get it looked at. We'll go to the hospital right away.

I'm not listening to her. I'm thinking about the girl, about her seafoam eyes, and the way she pulled me off the ground and kept me going when she didn't have to. The way the beast devoured her instead of me.

It should have been me.

It's the thought that forces my hands to the wheelchair's armrests. If I really can walk again, if I'm not imagining all of this, I won't sit here...won't leave this place hobbled and broken. Not when the price for my legs was her life.

With a heavy heart, I force my quads to contract and my arms to straighten, the girl's face still burning hot in my mind. And I stand.

YOU HAVE TO LET HIM BURN

The flight attendant cycled through her announcements—seat belts, oxygen masks, emergency exits—and Evelyn Walbrun patted Bennett's knee. "Buckle up, buddy."

He glanced up from his iPad with a groan, his dense, chocolate curls so like Trent's that it sometimes hurt to look at him. "Ahh, man, do I have to?"

"Yes. You do. Now, give me that thing." She took the iPad and ruffled his hair. "You can have it back once we take off, okay?"

"Fiiine," Bennett said. He straightened his legs and clicked the buckle, his eyebrows rising as he surveyed the cabin. "Wow, I can't believe we're actually gonna fly in this thing!"

Her stomach dropped, and she forced a smile. His first time, ever, on a plane. It should've been on a trip to Disney World or somewhere tropical. Not *this*. Anything but *this*.

Behind him through the window, a man in a hunter-orange vest waved a matching pair of wands. The plane nudged back and taxied for the runway. Evelyn exhaled and let her shoulders loosen. After six months of hell, they were finally leaving... finally putting the fire behind them. All the pain and heartache. Everything they'd lost. *Everyone.* Not that she truly believed that; she knew that wasn't how grief worked, but it was worth a shot. And California was as far from Boston as you could get.

Bennett laid his head on her arm, and she took his hand and traced her thumb over his palm, his wrist. In a way, his burns were beautiful; the pink and white swirls reminded her of the paintings she often stumbled across while perusing the art galleries on Newbury Street. The abstract pieces that looked like someone had opened a vein and emptied all their emotion onto the canvas in a blaze of color. All their hate. All their love. At times, the paintings left her breathless. They were perfect as they were, the same as Bennett. The fire hadn't changed that. Nothing would.

An announcement squelched through the speakers, and she tipped her head back against the seat and closed her eyes. She was asleep before the wheels left the ground.

Like always, Evelyn dreamed of Trent, his chin covered in stubble, his eyes like lake water at dawn. That familiar half-grin with one corner ending in a dimple. The way his hair tousled with sleep. How, when she ran her fingers through it, it sparked and caught, the fire blooming brighter, engulfing his head in a blue corona of flame. The low rising wail that pulsed up his throat before his lips turned to ash.

"…get you anything?"

Evelyn's eyelids fluttered open to a weary, customer-service smile and a warm pair of eyes. The flight attendant: hand wrapped around a notepad, nails perfectly manicured, one foot tapping away. *Hurry up, lady, people are waiting.*

"I'm sorry?" Evelyn asked.

"Would you like something to drink?"

"Oh, no I'm good, thank you. Bennett, how about you?" She reached for him and felt empty fabric. "Bennett?" She blinked the sleep from her eyes and squinted back at the flight attendant. "He must have gone to the bathroom. How about a ginger ale for him?"

"For whom, ma'am?"

"My son."

"I don't recall anyone sitting next to you. Is he perhaps in another seat?"

"No, he was right here next to me when I fell asleep."

"Are you sure? I didn't see anyone."

A sudden flare of heat filled her chest. "Yes, of course, I'm sure. It's my child we're talking about here."

The flight attendant's cheeks flushed, and she fingered her collar bone.

Evelyn exhaled. "I'm sorry, I didn't mean to snap at you. He's probably in the restroom." She looked behind the flight attendant as she said it, toward the front of the cabin. The bathroom sign glowed green. Another glance toward the lavatories in the back, and she saw one was unoccupied, the other taken. That had to be Bennett. Where else would he be?

She stood and squeezed past the woman into the aisle. "Excuse me."

"Ma'am," the flight attendant called after her, "please sit down. The captain hasn't turned off the seatbelt sign."

Evelyn ignored her and strode for the back of the plane and knocked on the door. "Bennett? Bennett, are you in there?"

"It's taken." The reply came muffled and gruff. Full of bass—a man's voice.

She turned and opened the other door. Empty—just a toilet lid spotted in urine. She closed her eyes and forced herself to think. If he wasn't here, he had to be in the bathroom near the cockpit. *Had* to be. He'd probably just spaced locking the door. Bennett was nothing if not forgetful. He often left his backpack at school, not to mention his water bottle and jacket.

She hurried back down the aisle and bumped the flight attendant, who was busy handing a cup of coffee to a man with a belly that brushed his tray. A slug of the steaming liquid slopped onto his gut, and he yelped and flapped at his shirt. "Ouch. Shit, lady! Watch where you're going!"

"I'm sorry," Evelyn sputtered over her shoulder without stopping. All that mattered was finding Bennett.

A prayer whispered off her lips as she reached the front of the plane and jerked the bathroom door open. The light flashed. Empty. She caught a flicker of her face in the mirror. Her eyes were stained pink, the pads of skin beneath swamped black with mascara. A tear cut down her cheek, and she wiped at it angrily.

No, stop, she told herself. *Don't you do it, don't you cry.*

Overhead, an announcement squawked: *"Ladies and Gentlemen, we'll be experiencing some brief turbulence for the next few minutes. Please keep those seatbelts fastened and your tray tables locked."*

"Ma'am, I'm going to have to ask you to return to your seat."

Evelyn jolted and spun around. The man behind her stood at average height, dressed in a pair of creased slacks and an olive-green polo. His arms were crossed, and he stared at her with the no-nonsense look of an over-caffeinated cop, or a DMV employee after a long day.

Her hands trembled. "I can't. My son is missing. I fell asleep, and when I woke up, he was just…gone."

The man massaged his temples and sighed, fished a wallet from his pocket, and flipped it open to a badge that read John Lawton, Federal Air Marshall. He snapped it shut. "I just spoke with the flight attendant. She filled me in on what you said. Look, I've been over the manifest a couple of times now. There are five kids on this flight, and none of them belong to you. Here, see for yourself." He retrieved a phone and flashed her the screen, then tapped a name. *Her* name. "That's you, right? Evelyn Walbrun, thirty-five. Born November nineteenth. Brown hair and hazel eyes."

Her palms went slick. She smoothed her shirt. "This isn't possible. I'm telling you my son is on this flight. There has to be some sort of mistake. His name is Bennett. He's only six, and he does this sometimes when he gets nervous. Hides, I mean. He… he—" She stared at her son's empty seat. "He was right there a minute ago. I swear."

"Come on," John said, taking her by the elbow. "Let's go."

She didn't resist. She let herself be led like a child, John in front and tugging her down the aisle like she was floating, like she wasn't the one controlling her limbs. When they reached her seat, the air marshal cupped her shoulder and pressed down with a firm, but gentle pressure until she sat. It took her a moment to realize he was still speaking.

"Listen, you seem like a nice enough lady. Do us both a favor and behave, okay?" He cocked an eyebrow at her, and Evelyn jerked back. A glistening sea of heat blisters had consumed his face, and his eyes were spider-webbed red with veins. "Okay?" he repeated.

His lips were melting.

Slowly, and with great effort, Evelyn managed to nod, but not before she rubbed her eyes and glanced at him again. There he stood once more: John the air marshal looking as normal as ever, balding and broad-shouldered.

"Good. I'm glad we understand each other. You enjoy the rest of your flight, Mrs. Walbrun. I'll be keeping an eye on you."

Rings of heat broke across the back of her neck as he left, and she looked across the aisle to a kid wearing a set of headphones that swallowed his ears. She recognized him: Dominique (but he went by Dom) Harris, who lived on the first floor of her building and had a penchant for late-afternoon strolls to the 7-Eleven in hunt of Slurpees. Behind him sat George and Margaret Shumway, both in their fifties and both with bad hearing. A few rows up, she spotted Calvin Foster, the skater kid with Kool-Aid-blue hair who lived in the apartment upstairs from her and beat on his drums until chips of plaster fell from the ceiling. And next to him, the landlord, Mr. Jameel, with the kindly face and whose voice never carried much bite, even when he meant it to.

Jake Gibbons, the building handyman, was the first to ignite. He flashed her his easy smile as candles of flame spread over his shoulders and threaded down his chest. Trails of smoke seeped from his ears. Alan Conroy caught next, followed by the Burtons, Susan staring at her with the aqua eyes Evelyn had always thought so beautiful. The eyes that were currently bubbling and oozing down her face in two viscous streams.

And then Evelyn was up and running, sprinting for the back of the plane, the captain announcing their descent into San Bernardino International, with the plane shifting in a way that nearly sent her tumbling backward. The acrid scent of burning hair and the sweet tang of boiling blood stung her nostrils. Fingers reached for her, blackened nails scraping across her forearms and neck. A hand wound around her wrist, and she choked back a cry but managed to pull loose as John Lawton moved to stop her. Bright rivers of flame chewed through his torso and bled down his hips.

"Hey, I thought we had an underst—"

Evelyn tucked her shoulder and rammed him at full speed. He toppled in a column of smoke. She leaped over him…and stopped. There he stood, Bennett, cowering against the back wall of the galley with his eyes screwed shut and his hands glued to his ears.

"Make it stop, make it stop, make it stop," he whimpered.

She took him in her arms and slammed into the bathroom, locking the door behind her. She ran her hands over his face, over his arms and legs, in search of burn marks, of which there were none, *thank God,* save for the ones she knew by heart. Then, she was thumbing his tears and struggling not to cry herself.

"Are you okay, baby? Please tell me you're okay."

His mouth trembled, and he managed to nod before collapsing into her chest. She held him there, feeling his breath warm a circle in her shirt—her son who was still alive, who'd been on the plane this entire time, hidden away, too scared to come back to her for fear that these *things*, whatever they were, would seize him before he could.

A knock rattled the door, followed by John's voice. "Mrs. Walbrun. Mrs. Walbrun, you need to come out. For your own good." He spoke in a tone reserved for a five-year-old. She suddenly had the urge to open the door and strangle him. Instead, she bit her tongue and went silent.

And then she heard it; the voice she knew so well. It filled her like a song, the same as it had every day for the last twelve years until the fire had burned it away.

"Evy, it's okay. You can open the door."

Her throat thickened. Bennett glanced over his shoulder. "Daddy?"

It ripped a hole in her heart, the way his face flushed and his eyes lightened. It carved out her soul. But still, Evelyn didn't reach for the door because she knew that whatever was speaking to her from the other side wasn't her husband.

Trent was dead.

"Please, Evy. Please, come out."

Smoke curled in around the doorframe and settled against the ceiling. Beads of sweat swamped her forehead and stung her eyes. She wrapped her arms around Bennett. Trent's voice was swallowed by others, their shouts rising in pitch and turning angry.

"You come out here this instant!" Margaret Shumway wailed.

"You belong with us!" George echoed. "Quit hogging the bathroom!"

"Please don't let them in, Momma," Bennett said. "Please."

John's voice followed. "Mrs. Walbrun, I've contacted the authorities. They'll be waiting when we land. But if you come out now, I'll see what I can do to make this go away. If you stay in there any longer...well, things will be a lot harder to handle."

She had to be hallucinating. *Had to be.* Her therapist said it happened sometimes with trauma. That in situations like these—

A heavy thud hammered against the door. Another. It buckled near the bottom, and a set of fingers wrapped around the metal and pushed inward. A head snaked through the opening, followed by a pair of black-socket eyes, and a nose burned to the sinuses. The landlord, Mr. Jameel.

"Stay with us!" he hissed. "We're your family now."

Bennett shrieked, and Evelyn pulled him behind her, ready to send her heel into what was left of the man's face, but before she could, the unmistakable squeal of rubber on asphalt sent her flailing into the sink, followed by the sound of thrusters in reverse.

"Ladies and gentlemen, welcome to hell. It's a wonderful day outside. Local time is just after two p.m. with a temperature right around ten thousand degrees. Please stay seated with those buckles fastened. We'll arrive at the gate in just a few minutes."

Evelyn winced and fingered a lump behind her ear. Bennett cried beside her, his breath coming in sharp bursts. She tilted his chin up and clasped his face.

"Baby...baby, look at me. You're fine. But we can't stay here. We have to go."

His cheeks paled. "No, no, no, they'll get us, I know they will!"

"Who are you talking to in there?" John asked.

A steady billow of smoke filled the cramped space. It smelled like beef frying, or a mix of pork and rendered fat. Only sweeter, the taste of it seeping into her mouth all the way to the root of her tongue.

"Hey, *hey*, I'm scared, too," she said. "But we can't stay here. We have to be brave. Both of us. Can you do that, for me? Can you be my brave little guy for just a little bit longer?"

His lower lip wobbled in the way it used to after he woke from a night terror.

"Okay, Momma."

"Good boy." She lifted his shirt over his mouth and pressed his hand over it. "Once we start, you don't stop, Bennett. You run. Even if I fall, you run. Even if you can't see me. Do you understand? You run until you are off this plane."

He gave her a weak nod.

"Let's go." She gripped his hand, opened the door...

And they ran.

Evelyn jerked Bennett forward, past John Lawton, who lunged for her with fingers that were scorched to the bone. He snagged her shirt, but she managed to rip loose, and they charged down the aisle through clouds of whirling cinder.

"Mrs. Walbrun! Mrs. Walbrun, stop!"

She glanced over her shoulder at the air marshal and went dizzy. He suddenly looked...normal, the cabin once again bright and airy. On either side of him, people gawked at her open-mouthed. A child close to Bennett's age tugged on his mother's shirt and pointed. A lip-glossed teenager in the adjacent seat laughed and filmed her with a cell phone.

Evelyn blinked, and the people turned to charred strips of flesh.

John Lawton strode toward her, clutching a pair of flaming handcuffs. "Mrs. Walbrun!"

She gasped and yanked Bennett onward, sparks singeing her shoulders, her scalp. Bennett screeched and slapped at his neck.

"It hurts! Ow, ow, it hurts!"

Ahead, she spotted a weak square of sunlight cracking open.

The door to the jetway, she realized. She pulled Bennett faster and tasted fresh air—felt it slide cool across her skin. They were going to make it!

The thought died as two monstrous figures in white uniforms pressed into the plane. One had ears melted to the lobes, the other eyelids that flagged and drooped like the eyelets of a rubber mask. He seized her by the torso, the other man by her arm. White bands of heat ripped across her chest and scorched her bicep, sending a shriek racing up her throat.

"Let her go!" Bennett cried.

Evelyn grasped his hand, gasping and choking, fighting to hold on, to never let go, until, with a violent jerk, his fingers tore from hers. Fingers which, she now saw, were glowing red with veins of fire. His mouth stretched wide in a howl as she bucked to reach him, twisting and scratching at the arms restraining her until they wrenched her out onto the jetway.

"Jesus, this lady is strong!"

"Yeah, no shit! Get her down already."

The pressure around her midsection increased, and her knees buckled. A hand ripped her arm halfway up her back, a bolt of pain shredding through her shoulder.

"Hey! What the hell are you two doing? Jesus, take it easy. You'll break her arm!" The force on her back relaxed, and Evelyn looked up to John Lawton crouched in front of her with his elbows perched on his knees. He rubbed his eyes and sighed. "I told you this would happen, didn't I? Dammit, why do you people make me do this shit?" He glanced at the men holding her. "Get her off the floor."

Behind him, through the plane's doorway, Bennett watched her stand. A hand rested on his shoulder, the fingers black with ash. A face materialized above it, the features cracked and fissured with heat lines. A face whose shape she knew by heart... every angle, every curve. Trent's eyes were blue points of flame as they tipped lower toward Bennett. *"Evelyn, you have to let him go. You have to let him burn."* His gaze lifted to hers. *"Evy, you have to remember."*

And she did.

Pushing through the sea of panicked faces crowding their building, the people's features smudged as though they'd been painted in watercolor. The towering inferno above her belching dark sheets of smoke. The windows on the fourth floor blowing out, the glass misting down around her in a thousand glittering pieces. They were up there, burning, Trent and Bennett, because that's where she'd left them to run to the store for eggs. *A weekend breakfast would be nice,* she'd thought. *How wonderful for them to wake to the smell of frying bacon and fresh coffee.*

The memories flooded faster: her legs churning as she barreled for the entrance. The explosion of light behind her eyelids as she collided with someone. The bridge of her nose as it crunched. Running again, her nose pouring blood as she strained to catch sight of Trent's green windbreaker or Bennett's paw-print pajamas. Praying that if she didn't, she'd find the strength to rush into the building and burn with them.

And then she spotted Bennett near an ambulance, strapped to a stretcher with one charcoaled hand hanging off the side, the other resting on his chest, red and steaming. His name exploded off her tongue as she flew forward. *Bennett! Baby, I'm here!* He was alive, and she could feel him, and she knew. But then the EMT shook his head and pulled the sheet higher, and she fell to her knees. A cry lodged in her throat, and stomach acid filled her mouth.

Trent's voice came again, and the timbre of his words ran through her like a mouthful of warm cinnamon.

"Evy...Evy, he'll be okay. We both will."

And she saw by the way Bennett nuzzled close to him, by the way he stared up through the flames at his father, that Trent was right. He looked at her then, her dead husband, and pressed two ash-colored fingers to his lips. He held them there a moment before pulling them away in a kiss. Their goodbye—from the windows of the apartment, through the windshields of departing cars—*I love you.*

"Mrs. Walbrun. Mrs. Walbrun, can you hear me?"

John Lawton's voice bled through the haze, and his gray eyes materialized next, followed by a mouth pressed into a grim line. When she didn't answer, he reached out and took her by the shoulders. "Hey. Stay with me. Are you okay?"

Evelyn stared at him for a long moment before answering. "No," she whispered, glancing back at the plane, which was now white and fresh and new. "No, I'm not. But maybe in time."

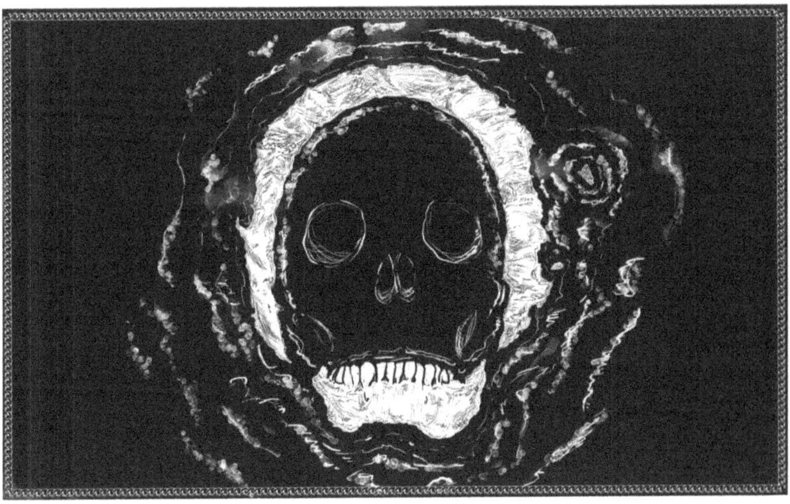

THE ATOLL

DAY ONE: DESOLATION

My arms are rivered with blisters as we heave the ruined life raft from the waves and slap it down on a pair of sun-bleached rocks. I cup a hand to my forehead and squint against the brilliant evening surf. It's hard to make out through the heat waves dancing off the ocean, but it's there in the distance: a fringe of green capping a pale, wave-battered coast. Palm trees and white sand; the thing I never thought I'd lay eyes on again. *An island.*

"I knew it," I whisper.

"Oh...my god," Alicia says next to me, her face a mess of peeling skin. "Eric, you were right."

"Little good it does us here," Patrick mutters. "Goddamn coral came out of nowhere."

He tugs his aviators lower, his eyes bloodshot and cupped in two pasty-white circles of flesh. "It's gotta be a couple miles to that island from here. Maybe more."

"What is this, anyway?" Alicia asks, surveying the thin strip of land we're beached on—an islet piled in rocks and sand and not much else, save a scattering of grass bunched along the tide in glistening pockets. "A sandbar or something?"

"No, an atoll." Patrick points over her shoulder toward a low stone ridgeline disappearing beneath the waves in spots and rising above them in others, looking like the spine of some enormous creature slithering through the surf. "See how it circles the island? There, there, and there? You're looking at an ancient volcano. And we're stuck on the rim."

We take shelter next to a low shelf of rock and watch the sun die a slow death on the horizon; an angry red eye drowned in a blaze of orange and yellow. Beneath it, the ocean is flat. A rippling, endless mirror, all of it one terrible display of beauty waiting to devour us like it did Hannah. Still, I can't help but think how much she would have loved this view—even now, here at the end of things.

God, it's so beautiful, Eric...isn't it?

The thought stirs an ache in my chest—a deep, throbbing loss like my heart has been carved out with a dull spoon.

"One of nature's cruelest jokes," Patrick says, ripping me from the thought.

I glance up. "What's that?"

"All this water, and not a drop to drink."

"At least we don't have to sleep on that awful raft again," Alicia says.

That awful raft. I grit my teeth at the comment, at the vanity of it here, now, in all of this emptiness, like she expects the ocean to raise Patrick's ruined yacht from its depths and return it to her unscathed.

The jab is out of my mouth before I can stop it. "You mean the thing that's kept us alive for the last two weeks?"

Her eyes harden, and she holds my gaze. She wants to tell me it's my fault, what happened to Hannah. She's wanted to since the boat went down. I can feel it every time she looks at me, hear it in her below-the-breath retorts. *(You would say that, wouldn't you?)* She thinks I'm the one who killed Hannah, not the sea…that I'm the one who fed her best friend to the waves.

Patrick groans. "Don't start, you two. Jesus. The last thing we need right now is more fighting. Here—" he digs in the raft and tosses me a water bottle, handing another to Alicia, "—go easy with it. Only a few left."

I catch the bottle and take a drink, the water spilling down my throat like a miracle. Another drink, and my thirst rises like gas on a fire and rages at me to down the entire bottle in one gulp. It's all I can do to cap it and save some for later. The two cases of water we wrestled into the raft before the yacht capsized have dwindled to nine bottles. Six after tonight's provision. A bottle a day per person, and no more. It's like I'm watching the countdown to my death in bottled water. Two days left...

Patrick reclines against the rock. "We should get some sleep while we can."

"Is it even safe to sleep here?" Alicia asks, eyeing the rising tide.

He waves at a pair of boulders near the break. "See that? We're above the salt line. The tide won't crest it. At least not tonight, anyway. Sea's calm."

Alicia relaxes and nuzzles in next to him, looking sun-scorched with her hair matted to her face in greasy strands. Even her eyes are burned, the sclera a cloudy, salmon pink. Patrick isn't much better off. His ribs are practically slicing through his shirt, his face hollow and gaunt. Still, I can't help but feel a sudden shot of jealousy; at least they have each other. All I have is the fading memory of Hannah flapping her arms beneath a white-foam mountain, her mouth stretched wide in a silent scream. Me screaming back—screaming until my throat tore.

I settle into the sand and stare up at the stars popping out in glittering bunches. There's something off about the memory, a piece missing. Hannah's hand in mine, me pulling, fighting to wrench her back into the raft. The terror flooding her eyes, her face. Something rippling behind her in the water...

God, why can't I remember?

The thought lingers as I close my eyes and chases me into an uneasy slumber.

I should be able to remember...

A riptide, dark and black, pulls me under. Frigid water thrusts into my mouth, my lungs, something in the deep singing to me, calling me lower...

I lurch awake with the breath of a drowned man, a sharp inhalation followed by two more. A gibbous moon drenches the atoll in a pure white light that looks like it was mined from bone. Beneath it, the ocean shines like black gloss cut with ribbons of moonlight...and something else, a deep throbbing glow floating through the waves.

What the hell?

I stand for a better look, convinced I'm delirious—that hunger and dehydration have finally taken their toll—but it's there all right, a soft, blue-green luminescence expanding and contracting through the water like a submerged heartbeat. Something about the motion sends flickers of static shooting through my vision and, before I know what I'm doing, I'm stumbling toward it, banging my feet against half-buried rocks, my shins cracking through dead spokes of coral. A voice hisses from the back of my skull to slow down, that I'm moving too fast, that I'll fall, *surely, I'll fall,* but it doesn't matter. Nothing does. Only reaching the shimmering pool of light in the water, the pulse somehow familiar and calling me closer.

The smell of salt fills my nose. A black rope of foam laps at my feet, the sea hissing over the sand and drawing back again in perpetual rhythm as I lurch for the glimmer of light. It spreads through the water in rich skeins of color, running over the ocean floor like a pad of butter rolling around a skillet. And all the while it thrums with a beat that mirrors the one thumping in my chest.

Bum...Ba-Bum...Bum.

The colors bleed around my feet. They're electric, unlike anything I've ever seen. Breathtaking blues and greens that shimmer above the seafloor like a cloud of gems. They swirl faster, brighter, a shape forming, a hand blooming from the haze followed by a set of frost-colored fingers. Hair…

"Eric?" Patrick's voice snaps me from the trance.

I turn, waves rolling over my thighs, my waist.

"What are you doing out there?"

I try to answer, but my tongue won't peel from the roof of my mouth. Sparks of light crash through my vision. I glance behind me for the glow, that strange, throbbing pulse, but it's gone...*or was it ever there?* The thought ignites a sudden sense of loss. A deep need to see it again. To *feel* it. I blink hard and grow vaguely aware of Patrick working to his feet.

"Hey, you okay, man?"

I wave him off and slosh back to shore, the sea frothing behind. Scrubbing the sand.

"I'm fine. Sorry to wake you"

He tilts his head. "You sure? You don't look fine."

"Yeah, I just needed to clear my head a bit. Couldn't sleep."

"Well, don't waste any more energy," he says, lying down again. "We need to fix the raft in the morning."

"Yeah, sure," I mutter, following suit. A headache clamps over the back of my neck as soon as my head hits the sand. Tendrils of pain creep behind my eyes, a storm gathering, and I'm left wondering if the glow was real or just some waking dream.

DAY TWO: DELIRIUM

Steam bakes off the rocks in waves. I kneel next to Patrick with the patch material, the sun pinned to the sky above us in a white-hot ball of heat. Beads of sweat roll down my back as Patrick spreads a thin layer of adhesive over the nylon and glances at me.

"So, what was that last night?"

"What?"

"The midnight dip?"

"Oh." *Play dumb.* "Like I said. Couldn't sleep."

He gestures at me for the patch, and I hand it to him. "Hannah again?"

"Yeah."

"Mm. Me, too." He smooths the patch over the six-inch gash and steps back with his arms crossed, the pits of his shirt stained a dark yellow. "There. That should do it."

"So, now what?" I ask.

"Now, we let it dry. And then we test it."

I rock back on my heels and look across the lagoon at the island, peering through a wet layer of haze. It reminds me of a painting. All earth tones with green oil brushstrokes smudged together in the shape of trees. They look dense and inviting. Lush. There's sure to be food there, and shade. *God,* what I'd give for some shade right about now. Here on this sun-blasted strip of rock, there's none, save a small stretch of it running beneath the stone shelf where Alicia and Patrick slept last night. Where Alicia is still dozing with an elbow cocked across her eyes and one lobster-red leg slung across the sand.

Patrick notices me looking at her and settles into a low crouch. "Maybe take it a little easier on her, huh?"

I wipe a pair of sweat prints on my shorts. "She thinks it's my fault."

"What?"

"Hannah."

"No, she doesn't. It's just...you know how close they were. Give her some time, she'll come around."

A bolt of anger cuts through me. He says it like she's the only one who's carrying the weight of Hannah's loss, like she's the only one who's lost something.

"Christ, Patrick, she was my *wife*. Don't you think I'm hurting here, too?"

He claps a hand on my shoulder, eyes creasing. "And she was my sister. My twin. Look, I know you're hurting. We all are. All I'm trying to say is—"

"—what? That I should have held on longer? Pulled harder?" The words threaten to unleash the sudden dam of tears welling behind my eyes. Tears I can't afford to shed, considering what little moisture is left in my body. I force my gaze to my hands and tell myself to hold it together, to stop the dramatics. "I did everything I could."

"Eric..."

I let my name hang there, heavy and awkward, my throat too tight to speak. Patrick leans back and wraps his arms around his knees, both of us sinking into the sudden silence. After a moment, he shakes his head.

"You know that's not what I mean, man. If I lost Alicia..." He sighs. "All I'm trying to say is, we need to stick together if we're going to survive this."

I get it. *Play nice.* "Okay," I mutter. "I'll try."

He squeezes my shoulder and stands. "Hang in there."

It's all I can do to nod.

We test the raft around noon. Patrick uses the foot pump to inflate the torn ballast tubes and then loops a length of rope around the handline and hands it to me.

"Here, in case I hit a current. I'll just do a quick test run, and then we'll head for the island. Sound good?"

I hold the line tight, and Alicia shoves the raft into the break. "Try to avoid the coral this time."

He flashes her a half-grin. "Very funny."

We wade into the water and unspool the rope as Patrick rows, making sure there's plenty of slack as he floats further into the lagoon. Alicia's eyes are wide and unblinking as she watches the raft glide over the waves. She knows it as well as I do: If this doesn't work, if the raft fails again, we're screwed.

"He'll be fine," I say. An attempt at reconciliation.

She offers me a weak smile. "I know. He always is."

"He's one hell of a seaman, that's for sure."

"The best."

And it's true. Without Patrick, we wouldn't have made it off the yacht, much less survived fifteen days in the open ocean with sharks nipping at the raft like it was a floating appetizer—the same as me and Alicia. We would have killed each other in two days without him there to calm us down.

She wraps her arms around her torso and rubs them as if she's standing in the middle of a snowstorm. I let out the rest of the rope, suddenly sorry for attacking her last night. She's scared like the rest of us, and Patrick is right that we need to stick together if we're going to make it through this.

"Listen, Alicia," I start. "About last night... I'm sorry. It's just been hard with—"

She raises a hand, her mouth in a knot.

"What is it?" I ask.

"Something's wrong. Look."

I follow her gaze to Patrick waving at us. He's a ways out now and gesturing wildly with his arms.

"What's he doing?"

"I think he wants us to pull him in."

Patrick cups his hands to his mouth in a shout. I should be able to hear him, but the only sound I can make out is the wind in my ears and the low, easy slosh of the ocean.

"Eric," Alicia prods, "please. Let's bring him in."

"Right. Okay. Let's do it."

She settles in behind me, and we heave on the rope. It goes taut, the raft floating in place like it's made of concrete. It doesn't move an inch.

"What the fuck?" I mutter.

"Pull harder," Alicia says, her voice rising a notch.

I nod, and we heave again to the same effect, the rope snapping into place like a steel cable, the raft inexorable, sitting there as though Patrick somehow anchored it to the seafloor. He spreads his arms like Alicia and I have no clue what we're doing before shouting again.

"What's that?" I call back.

"Why won't it move?" Alicia asks.

"I don't know. Here—" I brace my legs and my feet, loop the rope through my hands for a better grip "—let's give it another shot. On three. One. Two..." Before I can count it off, the rope rips forward, as if the raft is pulling back, and whips me face first into the water. A mouthful of brine pummels the back of my throat, and I come up coughing. Alicia is squealing next to me and staring at a nasty pair of friction burns cutting over her palms. Buttons of blood bubble up from the wounds and drip through her fingers. Her eyes find mine and rim with tears.

"Shit," I say, moving for her. "Here, let me have a look."

"What the *hell* are you two doing?"

Patrick's voice spins me around, and I nearly topple at the sight of the raft floating a few feet back, Patrick glaring down at us and swaying like an angry drunk. "You pulled so hard, you tore the patch!"

Tore the patch? I open my mouth to respond, but no words spill out. *It's impossible. There's no way we could have pulled that hard. And Patrick shouldn't be here. Not this close this fast.*

"Why didn't you let go of the rope?" he asks.

My jaw clicks into place. "You waved at us to pull you in."

His eyes narrow. “No, I didn’t. I was screaming for you to let go. You two started yanking me back before I even made it ten feet. Shit, that last tug nearly tossed me in the water.”

“Patrick, there wasn’t any rope left. We let it all out.”

A deep crease forms over the bridge of his nose. Somewhere behind me, Alicia moans, and the crease melts. “Oh, God.” He leaps from the raft and splashes by me to take her hands in his. “What happened?”

“W-we were trying to bring you in, and the rope...it—it just ripped us forward.” She looks up at him. “Patrick, Eric’s right. We let it all out. We weren’t pulling you back. You were out past the reef...and you pulled us.”

We take the sun canopy from the raft and stretch it from the stone shelf to the sand before anchoring it with several fist-sized stones. Storm clouds billow dark and formless on the horizon, lightning sparking down in great white columns. A gust of wind whips bits of sand into my face and scatters tracks of it along my arms and legs, tracks like those blistered across my skin by the sun. The temperature has dropped ten degrees, and I’m close to shivering, but not from the weather. Rather, from what I *saw:* Patrick paddling out past the break, the raft drifting out into the lagoon. Beyond him, the island looming in a blurry smear. That first, wild wave of his arms. Alicia and I pulling, heaving on the rope. The mad yank back, the rope ripping me forward into the water. Alicia’s cry. The raft somehow behind me, *right fucking behind me,* and Patrick fuming...

I’m losing my mind.

But I’m not, because Alicia saw it, too.

I grind the pads of my thumb and forefinger over my eyes. "What the hell are we going to do?"

Patrick stares dimly from his sun-leathered face, his usual easy confidence gone. He doesn't answer, and when I repeat the question, he runs a hand over his chin and looks at me like he's waking from a deep slumber.

"I...don't know. I need to think on it some. For now, we stay put. Conserve energy and get some sleep."

He hasn't said much since we pulled him in. There's something off in his clipped answers, like maybe he still thinks we...*I*... sabotaged him. That I wanted to keep us here, starving on this empty, sun-blasted patch of rock.

I lie back and close my eyes as the rain begins to fall in a soft, steady patter, the sound hypnotic against the canopy, and the air cool and comfortable on my ruined skin, a salve.

Sleep takes me before I know I'm gone.

I dream of Hannah, of her face. The shape of it, oval, her chin smooth beneath a pale set of lips. Her eyes are luminous as they sink beneath the waves and fade to two pale blue coins staring up at me from the depths. And then those are gone, too.

My eyelids snap open.

It's black out, and for a moment I think I'm back in Connecticut in the safety of my room with Hannah nuzzled warm beneath my chin. A cold drizzle brings me back, and I sit up in a rush, eyes wide. The ocean froths along the islet, stirred by the storm. I can't see much of it, but enough to make out the faint glimmer of frozen light rising and falling within the waves. There's something different about it tonight, though...a section obscured in the shape of a man. A shape I recognize: a broad set of shoulders and a pair of stiff arms. A head angled down toward the water. Staring...

Patrick. I pat the sand next to me and feel the empty cup of earth where he should be. Next to it, Alicia snores softly with her ruined hands folded on her chest. Again, I glance through the rain toward Patrick, who hasn't moved, hasn't looked up once, his shoulders heaving with each breath and his head bowed. I stand to shout, but there's something about his stance and the way he's gazing into the water, fists balled, that gives me pause.

I lie back down instead until I hear him near the tarp, and then pretend to sleep, keeping my eyes open in slivers. He crouches just beyond my feet and cocks his head like maybe he's thinking about doing something. What it is, I have no clue, but his posture, the way he's coiled there like a snake ready to strike, tells me it isn't good.

After a time, he slides in next to Alicia, and I watch him until his breathing evens out, then close my eyes and hope for sleep to take me. It's a futile pursuit. I lie there, awake and unsettled, until the sun crests the horizon and stains the clouds pink.

DAY THREE: ISLA DE LA MUERTE

I doze off sometime after dawn. When I wake, my eyes are grainy and dried out, my throat burning with thirst. I claw at a water bottle, one of three left, and down the entire thing before working my way out from under the canopy. It's a gray day, the ocean unsettled and choppy, churning up whitecaps along the tips of waist-high waves. Beyond them, the island hangs shrouded in mist, looking like the shell of some ancient tortoise.

A sudden stench fills my nose and pulls my gaze to the water, where the tide churns along the bank in dirty pockets of foam, bobbing off the break and rolling back in. Hundreds of bodies lie glittering across the sand. I narrow my eyes and struggle to believe what I'm seeing. *Fish.* Rows and rows of dead or dying fish. Their movement is all wrong as they flop along the shore in a collection of oily, gray-pink patches. They flail higher upon the beach in hitches and jerks as if they're trying to escape the water.

Further down, near a black jetty of rock, I spot Patrick and Alicia talking. Patrick jabs a finger in Alicia's face and points over the water, his teeth cutting a white line as he speaks. Alicia reaches for him, and he slaps her bandaged hand away and glances over her shoulder at me. The weight of his gaze renders me motionless, his eyes glowing like two burning coals.

He shoves past Alicia and marches my way, his finger out and pointing, mouthing a word clear even from a distance: "You." Alicia chases after him and grabs at his shoulder. He shakes her off, hard, and she falls, then regains her feet while yelling at him to stop.

Still, he comes, his attention squared on me, legs muscling forward in long, stern strides. I take a step back, confused, something in his face telling me I should run. I raise a hand instead and curl my lips into what I hope is a disarming smile.

"Patrick, you okay? What's the—"

I don't see the blow coming. Light webs behind my eyes as his fist connects with my temple. He hits me again, and my knees buckle. A wicked uppercut follows and sends me toppling to the ground. I look up through a shower of stars in time to see his fist arcing forward once more, and then I see nothing at all.

Moving.

I am moving. Sliding. No, that's wrong. Someone is dragging me, my body grinding over a bed of rocks. Sharp things chip at my feet and slice my ankles. There's a firm pressure, hands under my armpits, and I'm slumped against something hard. A looping tension slides around my chest. I struggle to open my eyes and fail...try again. Everything's a blur. Voices cut through the haze. A woman's and a man's, the woman pleading with the man, telling him, *No, no, please, God, noooo.* A hard thud, flesh on flesh. Another. A choking cry. I have to wake up. I need to—

Reality comes back in snatches.

A roiling, black sea.

The smell of salt and rotting fish.

Pressure around my waist, my wrists.

I can't move...can't reach up to extinguish the itch burning over my scalp or down to quell the one ravaging my leg. A low moan parts my lips.

"You had to answer them. *Why* did you have to answer them?"

The voice worms its way into my brain from some faraway place. I crane my head toward the sound, one eye swollen shut, and find Patrick perched nearby on a piece of driftwood, looking at me with all the compassion of a shark.

He's tied me to a boulder, coils of rope strung around my chest, my hands. My legs are splayed toward the water, which is several yards below my feet, though I know it won't stay that way forever, and certainly not through high tide. A splash of fear washes over me, and my tongue sparks to life.

"Patrick...wh-what...the fuck, man?"

He doesn't answer. Only gazes back at me with his beard hanging in wild strings. His eyes have lost their anger, replaced with something decidedly colder: a decision made.

I test the weight of the rope and try to free my hands. It's impossible. He's bound them in surgeon knots.

"Untie me."

He blinks. "You've damned us, Eric."

"What?"

"The night the boat went down, you heard them cry out, didn't you? For Hannah."

"I didn't hear anything... Jesus, Patrick, what the hell are you talking about?"

"They told me you would lie."

"They?" I echo. "You mean Alicia?"

He shakes his head. "You heard them cry out, you opened your ears, and you fed them my sister."

My jaw throbs, and I work it open and shut in clicks. I need to figure out what he wants, why he's done this. A blue slice of fabric further down the beach kills the thought. A racerback tank top. Beneath it, a familiar pair of legs lying crumpled to the side. I look back at him with a hard swallow.

"Patrick...where's Alicia?"

He cracks a knuckle, but says nothing.

I repeat the question.

"Resting." He cracks another knuckle. And another.

"Oh god, Patrick, what have you done?"

He shoots to his feet, lines carving through his forehead. "What have I done?" he snarls. "*Me?* No, Eric! No. Ask yourself. What have *you* done? What, exactly, have you done?" His lips are flecked with spit, his fists clenched and trembling, and I know if I answer wrong, he'll kill me this time.

Tread carefully. "Honestly, I have no clue what you're—"

"Hannah! I'm talking about Hannah, goddammit! They sang for her, and you answered!"

The missing memory clicks into place like a thunderbolt. The ocean crashing and booming against the yacht, Hannah's mouth open and screaming at me to pull her into the raft. *"Eric, don't let me go! Please, don't let go!"* Her hand in mine, slipping, her eyes turning slick with fear. Then, the light rising behind her—that faint, blue-green glow rippling through the waves. A voice in my head...no, *voices*...a legion of them urging me to let her go, to feed her to the waves.

And I let her go.

I buckle against the boulder, suddenly limp. *Oh, my god.*

Patrick's eyebrows arch. "Ahh, now you remember."

I feel myself nod, the weight of what I've done pinning me to the stone.

I killed my wife.

I sit reeling for hours, unable to speak. Unable to move.

I killed my wife. I let her go.

The sun bathes me in its radiation, burns over my skin as if focused through a giant magnifying glass. Strings of sweat turn to steam and rise off my shoulders to mingle with the stench of spoiled fish. It's grown unbearable, a sour odor trapped at the back of my throat. And none of it matters.

I killed Hannah.

Patrick sits next to me on the log, staring dead-eyed at the island, unmoving and silent, because he's killed his wife, too.

Near evening, I become aware of the water creeping closer to my feet, the color no longer green, but now a pale gray, its consistency murky and dense. Fish wash from the current and over the beach, one a swordfish with its brilliant scales blackened by something moss-like, its gills whooshing in and out in useless gasps. I look at it and wonder if that's how Hannah felt when she took in that last cold lungful of water. Frightened and alone. Confused. My eyes burn at the thought, and I would cry if I had any tears left, but I don't, so I just sit there, cold and shivering, and wait for the tide to take me.

"Not long now," Patrick says. It's the first time he's spoken in hours, the sun cutting a pink sliver over his shoulder. "They'll come for us soon."

"Who?"

"The dead."

I squint at him. *The dead?* "Patrick, don't do this. Untie me."

"It won't help. We belong to them now."

"What does it matter, then? C'mon, man. This isn't you."

"Did you give Hannah a choice?"

"Did you give Alicia one?"

His eyes turn to dark slits, and he glares at me. "Don't."

"Why? Who made you judge and jury? Untie me."

His jaw hardens, and he stands and points at the island. "You did, Eric. *You* did. The second you gave them Hannah. They won't let us leave now. What I did for Ali, I did out of love." His mouth bunches, and he wipes at his eyes. "They can't have her now. They *won't* have her."

"And you made sure of that, didn't you? You didn't give her a choice. You're a murderer, Patrick. A wife-killer just like me. Now untie me, you bastard!" I spit the words at him like a mouthful of acid.

He whirls on me, tendons ripping across his neck, his fist up and cocked.

"You sonofa—"

The rock comes down hard across the back of his skull. His eyes widen, and a thread of drool leaks from his lower lip. He blinks hard and then crumples to the side, his head cracking off a buried spur of stone. Alicia stands perched behind him with tears streaking her face, her skin the color of chalk.

"Alicia!" I say, straining to reach her, bucking against the rope. "Alicia, thank god. You have to untie me before—"

She lurches sideways with a groan. Her forehead is a crust of dried blood, fresh streams of it spilling from beneath her hairline and over her brow. Her pupils are dilated, shivering in place as her lips part to say something. All that comes out is a low, keening gurgle before she collapses to the sand.

The break rises and reaches my ankles first before sliding cold toward my knees. Alicia lies motionless beside Patrick, both of them staring up at me with dead eyes. Across the slate-colored water, the island looms dark and thick, trees circling it in a dense green skirt.

A sudden sob works its way up my throat. All I want is to rewind time back to the day Hannah came bounding into the kitchen with that daybreak smile splashed over her face—*"Guess what? We're going sailing!"*—and tell her that, no, no way in hell are we doing that. We're staying put, right there in our house where it's safe because I know what happens if we don't.

Grief engulfs me, and I sit there spinning in its depths as the water creeps ever higher—at my waist now—a memory ripping through my mind. The day I met Hannah at that stupid coffee shop downtown, her gasp as she bumped into me. *"Oh, I'm sorry..."* And then that smile like a sunrise. Me scooping up her cup and offering to buy her another one, knowing even then that there was something special about this girl.

The thought sets me to bucking against the ropes, straining and ripping, desperate to wriggle out of the knots. It's useless, even with as slick with my blood as my binds are now. Patrick tied them too well and with too much precision.

One hell of a seaman, I think dully.

When the moon breaks above the horizon, I'm close to freezing, so cold that I can barely snatch a breath. Strands of seaweed lick at my calves. Slick things dart around my thighs and into my shorts before squirming out again. Flies ravage my neck and bite my eyelids as the water rises. It curls beneath Patrick first, then Alicia. They float face down with their arms outstretched and their fingertips brushing as if in a final embrace. Dread clogs my throat. I know I'll soon join them, and I don't want to die like this. *Not like this.* Alone and roped to a rock in the middle of the ocean, soon to drown beneath it.

Like Hannah.

Something ripples across the lagoon; a deep, unearthly blue-green throb that bleeds through the water like a cloud of smoke. Terror spills down my spine, and I think of the hand and those frost-colored fingers. That dark cloud of hair. I screw my eyes shut and pray for whatever god is listening to save me. It's a messy, frantic prayer—the words frothing over my lips like water through a broken dam.

Please, God, please if you're up there, save me. Or kill me quick.

As if in answer, a deafening crack splits the air. An earth-rending sheering unlike anything I've ever heard. My eyes rip open to the whoosh and rumble of water pulling back, thinning. A mountain of sea spray pounds my face, my arms. There's a vast sucking sensation, a distortion of space as if I'm being wrenched forward over some great distance. And then I'm looking at the impossible.

The island.

The island lying right in front of me, now separated by twenty yards of water.

A belt of gleaming black sand.

Palm trees scraping off one another, their leaves whooshing in time with the wind. Creepers, knotted and thick, wrapping around their trunks. Climbing toward branches draped in long beards of moss.

And deeper, hidden somewhere in the pitch, are pockets of emerald light shining out.

Growing brighter.

Pulsing.

Ethereal shapes glide from the bracken onto the sand, their movements stuttered and halting. It takes a moment for my brain to piece them together, what exactly it is I'm looking at. A sight that doesn't make sense.

Corpses. Dozens and dozens of corpses.

They slide from the trees in groups of twos and threes, then more, their numbers growing until all I can make out is a glowing wall of shredded skin. Their mouths are slung open, black caves uttering words I can't understand. *They're singing,* I realize, as a harsh, biting melody carries over the wind and digs into my ears. The words grow louder and scrape across my eardrums, burrow into my veins and fizz hot in my blood.

The corpses reach the tide and sway there with distended jaws and eyes so black that I wonder if they're sockets. They sing louder, and a sudden rage swirls through my chest, a primal *need* to consume something. *Anything.* I watch, transfixed as one of the things sets upon Patrick's corpse with teeth like diamonds.

The resulting crunch sends a fountain of bile racing up my throat. The others join in, swarming over Alicia and Patrick like ants over a carcass. Ripping. Tearing.

Their howls rise and pitch into a terrible cacophony that reverberates through my head as waves of brine wash into my mouth. I spit it out with a cough, and one of the things lifts its head in response. It's a woman, if one could call her that, with strands of hair sprouting from a cracked skull. She stands and lumbers toward the water—followed by a pair of children, a boy in a tattered doublet and a girl wearing a moth-eaten gown.

The woman stops at the water and cocks her head in my direction, the children sniffing at the air behind her like a pair of dogs, their faces pocked with holes through which cords of rotten muscle and decayed tendon gleam.

"No," I hear myself whisper. *"No, no, no."*

The woman spots me and bounds forward with a hiss. The children follow, all three of them surging through the water in awkward, heaving leaps, their mouths packed with those awful diamond teeth.

They are no more than a foot away when a high, wailing lament brings them to a halt. A figure emerges from the trees, a woman with a black cloak of hair obscuring her face. She screams again, and the things turn and scatter back to the beach. She passes them and slips into the waves in a smooth fashion that's unlike the movement of the others…something closer to human in the way she walks.

As she nears, I make out a set of slender shoulders and ivory skin glittering with phosphorescent flecks of blue and green. My heart crashes like a caged bird as her hands rise to part the dark wall of hair dripping over her face.

I stifle a cry.

"Hannah?"

"Hello, my love."

Her voice slides into my ears slow and soft, as if carried there by the breeze. She's so close, I can see the water dewing on her forehead.

Something cracks within me—a feeling beyond grief, a heavy yearning to slip my binds and pull her into my arms and never let go. *Never, so long as I live.* But the woman I loved was blonde with green eyes, and this *thing* in front of me, *this* version of Hannah, is staring back at me through ice-colored eyes set deep within a face of pearl.

"How?" I whisper.

Her lips curl into a glimmer of a smile. She gestures at the creatures scattered on the beach picking over remains of Patrick and Alicia. "They needed me. They needed us."

"Hannah, I'm...so sorry. I—I..." My voice cracks. "God, how I've missed you."

She leans in and cups my chin. Her hands are like ice, her fingers cold and lifeless.

"And I, you."

The tide rises, nearing my chin. "I-I don't understand. What is this?"

She places a finger to my lips. "We're home. They," she says with a wave toward the things watching us from the sand, "are our family now."

The water ebbs higher, over my mouth, and I fight to pull in air through my nose. Hannah stays level with me, running a frigid hand through my hair.

"Breathe," she says. "All you have to do is breathe."

I shake my head, panic leeching into my bloodstream as the waves rise and swallow me whole. I jerk against the knots and scream, the ropes slicing against my wrists and legs. Bubbles cloud my vision, my brain screaming for oxygen, for air. I grind my eyes shut. Hannah reaches out and cups my face, and I open them.

She's there, floating with me, her hair hanging in the water like strands of black silk. With a smile, she presses her lips to mine and holds them there until the last few bubbles of oxygen work from my lungs and up my throat.

Breathe, she mouths, pulling back again. *Breathe.*

And with a final, deep inhalation, I do.

ACKNOWLEDGEMENTS

As a child, somewhere around third or fourth grade, my father handed me a little book by the name of *The Hobbit*. I was reluctant to read it at first. It seemed, to me at least, to be a rather large novel—far bigger than my previous book: Scott Odell's *Island of the Blue Dolphins* (which is another fantastic read). A novel that large was intimidating, but it also felt special in a way. The weight of it, the cover with Gollum peering so wickedly over Bilbo's shoulder. I had to crack it open.

Needless to say, I devoured it, lost in Tolkien's magical world of hobbits and goblins, wizards and warriors. It was this seed from which sprouted a passion for the written word, one that grew from there as I devoured works by Alan Dean Foster, and Terry Brooks, and C.S. Lewis. Later came Madeleine L'Engle, Robert Ludlum, and of course the horror master himself, Stephen King. I read and I read and I read.

And I loved every minute of it.

The first time I had an inclination to write something of my own occurred over beers with a close friend in a small bar in Fort Collins, Colorado. We were college juniors at that time, close enough to graduation to feel the weight of our impending futures creeping ever closer, and I mumbled something about wanting to write. *I think I'd like to be an author.* I don't know why I remember that moment, nothing substantial came from it—no short stories or novellas, certainly no novels—but something about that statement felt cosmic. *I want to write.* Yes, what a nice dream that would be.

And a dream it remained. I graduated with a marketing degree, and then, a few years later, tacked on an accounting degree for good measure. I worked hard to build a career, often putting in eighty hours a week in pursuit of corporate success. And, by most standards, I achieved that success. By my late twenties, I was solidly ensconced in my career and had built a nice, comfortable life with a new home and a wonderful family.

But, despite all of this, I felt like something was missing.

Writing...you are supposed to write.

The itch returned. I tried my hand at a novel, spent years in isolation penning it in the 5 a.m. margins of my life. I had a young family and a demanding career. It was difficult, but I kept writing, kept putting one word in front of another, stacking up sentence after sentence, until I keyed the two most important words an author can type: "The End." Those words were powerful, even if the book, upon reading it, wasn't exactly a masterpiece. Even though it took five long years to reach that point. I'd done the impossible. I'd finished a novel.

Unsure what to do next, I penned a short story. And then I wrote several more. They were a fun diversion, I thought, these shorts. A way to kill the time and improve my craft in between writing books. I kept at them in bunches and bursts, submitting them to literary magazines and anthologies, and a few podcasts here and there. The rejections stacked up, but I didn't much care. After all, I was a novelist, wasn't I? That's where I was really heading.

But after a while, something funny happened. A story of mine was accepted. A short was turned into a podcast. People started reaching out—on a rare basis, mind you—to share with me that they enjoyed what I'd written, that it meant something to them. Which meant something to me. A director in Los Angeles called, and I worked with him on a screenplay for several years. We made a short film, and I landed a literary agent. My next novel went on submission. All good things. But in between the success came long stretches of rejection, books that didn't sell and submissions that received form rejections—*I'm afraid this piece isn't quite what we're looking for.*

Rejection stings. Let me tell you, writing is no easy feat. It takes guts. It's riddled with heartbreak and drenched in defeat. And of all the voices, the harshest is often your own. *You can't do this,* you tell yourself. *You aren't good enough by a mile.* Which is why you can't do it alone, something that took me far too long to figure out.

I have so many people to thank. Thank you to my wife, Jennifer. You are the best person I know, and my very *favorite* person. Without you, I'd be lost. My parents. You poured your love of reading into me at a young age and allowed it to become my own. I am who I am today because of you. My daughters are always an inspiration. Know that the three of you are the stars that light my sky. And of course, a thank you to my sisters, Nicole and Elise, for putting up with me, and my writing, for all of these years. I appreciate you so very much.

To all the writers who've taken the time to read my work, and to pick me up when I'm down, this collection is for you. A special thanks to Charles Dunphey, Solomon Forse, P.L. McMillan, Shane Hawk, Evelyn Freeling, Jennifer Collins, Molly Halstead, Chris O'Halloran, C.B. Jones, Tina Alberino, Patrick Barb, Ai Jiang, and Christi Nogle. You know what you've done to help me along the way. And to everyone else, all my friends on Discord, Twitter, and scattered elsewhere across the Internet, know that even if I didn't thank you by name, your support is drizzled across these pages and baked into these stories.

And last, a thank you to you the reader for picking up this book and taking a chance on me. In the end, it's all I've ever wanted—to create worlds for others, places where they can leave their cares and worries behind, if only for a little while.

With that, I'm signing off. Until next time. I have more stories to write.

ABOUT THE AUTHOR

Caleb Stephens is a dark fiction author writing from somewhere deep in the Colorado mountains. His short stories have appeared in multiple publications and podcasts, including *Chilling Tales for Dark Nights*, *Tales to Terrify*, *MetaStellar*, *The Dread Machine*, *Nocturnal Transmissions*, and more. His story "The Wallpaper Man" was recently adapted to film by Falconer Film & Media. You can sign up for his mailing list and learn more at www.calebstephensauthor.com and follow him on Twitter @cstephensauthor.

Sign up for Caleb's mailing list!

To see the content warnings for this collection, please visit https://www.calebstephensauthor.com/if-only-a-heart-content-warnings or follow the QR Code below.

PUBLICATION HISTORY

"The Wallpaper Man" *Hinnom Magazine Issue 004*, December 2017

"I Will Wait for You" *Drunken Pen Writing*, October 2020

"If Only A Heart" *Suspense Magazine Vol. 086*, October 2019

"Welcome to Camp Klehani" *Mixtape 1986*, The Dread Machine, April 2022

"The Crowing" *Howls from the Dark Ages*, HOWL Society Press, May 2022

"Shadow Puppets" *The Dread Machine Vol. 1.1*, February 2021

"The Backward Man" *Night Terrors Vol. 7*, Scare Street, December 2020

"A Slide Infinite" *Night Terrors Vol. 8*, Scare Street, December 2020

"The Atoll" *The Dread Machine Vol 1.3*, September 2021

CPSIA information can be obtained
at www.ICGtesting.com
Printed in the USA
LVHW012049191122
733278LV00035B/1912

9 798985 871326